Sweet Adeline

By
Evelyn Allen Harper

Ink Smith Publishing
www.ink-smith.com

Sweet Adeline
By Evelyn Allen Harper

Formatted by V.J.O. Gardner
Cover By J. Alton. Mast
Edited By Corinne Anderson

The final approval for this literary material is granted by the author.
Printed in the U.S.A, 2016

ISBN: 978-1-939156-75-4

Ink Smith Publishing
710 S. Myrtle Ave Suite 209
Monrovia, CA, 91016

www.inksmith.com

To Sweet Adelines International

the organization that has filled my life with music
and friendships.

Table of Contents

Chapter 1

Where was Steve?

Adeline Parker tried not to look impatient, but keeping her excitement contained was getting harder by the minute. Trying to ignore her pinched toes that were complaining about her choice of shoes, she stepped side to side while scanning the lunch crowd streaming by.

She hadn't seen him since last Friday just before he left to go to a weekend high school reunion. Since he had tears in his eyes when they'd parted, she was puzzled that he hadn't contacted her as soon as he'd gotten back into town.

For days before he left for the reunion they'd agonized about being away from each other for the entire weekend. He didn't really want to go, he'd told her, but the other three in his singing group, "The Naked Four," were going to be there. The four had found while showering in the locker-room after a football game there was one song they could harmonize on. For the remainder of their high school years, they'd sung the chorus of *Sweet Adeline* at every occasion, even when it wasn't requested.

Her eyes filled with tears remembering how tenderly he'd kissed her after he'd sung the song to her in his rich baritone voice. Holding her close, he'd whispered, "The guys are always so jealous when I remind them that I have a Sweet Adeline of my own! Addie, I'll think about you every second of every minute of every day."

Where was he? It was twenty minutes past noon and now her toes were *really* objecting to the green shoes that matched her green outfit and her green eyes.

*****

She'd waited until late in the day on Monday before she called his cell, and when he didn't answer, she called his office.

"Steve Young's office, how may I help you?"

"Miss Snyder, this is Adeline Parker. Could I please speak to Mr. Young?"

"Oh, Miss Parker, hello! I'm glad you called. Mr. Young left a message for you."

"He did? Is he all right?"

"Oh, he sounded quite fine when he called! There was a lot of giggling going on in the background."

Giggling? Steve doesn't giggle. "Is he in town?"

"No, but he will be. His message to you is to meet him on Wednesday at noon outside Joe's Bar and Grill."

"Did he say anything else?"

"Yes, he did. He said, "Tell her I have something important to ask her.""

Addie's voice went up an octave. "He said that?"

"Yes, he did. I repeated it back to him to make sure I had it right."

"Oh, thank you, Miss Snyder, thank you! Bye."

Feeling giddy, Addie had sat with her phone in her hand, a big smile on her face, and joy in her heart. It was going to happen; Steve was going to propose!

Chapter 2

Thirty minutes past noon and her toes didn't hurt anymore; dead toes don't feel anything. Her make-up along with her hair was suffering from the noon heat and on top of that, she had to pee.

Her thoughts went back to the phone call. Why hadn't he called her instead of leaving the message with his secretary? The reunion ended on Sunday, so why was he going to be out of town until Wednesday? But knowing her beautiful and wonderful Steve as well as she did, she was sure that he'd have a very good reason for everything.

Taking a deep breath, she leaned against the wall of the restaurant and tried to relax. Steve was going to ask her to marry him and she'd wait as long as she had to. Holding out her left hand, she wiggled her ring finger, trying to imagine how it was going to look with an engagement ring on it.

While scanning faces as the stream of walkers passed by, her thoughts went to the actual proposal. Oh, it was going to be so exciting! Would he go down on one knee right here on the sidewalk, or would he wait until they were seated in the restaurant?

In her imagination, she pictured the scene. If it happened here on the sidewalk, the sight of her handsome Steve looking up at her with those love-filled blue eyes would certainly draw attention. In her mind's eye she chose to have a crowd gathering to wait for her answer.

Addie paused in her imagination. At this point in the proposal, should she go for an immediate acceptance or should she hesitate for a few seconds just to build up a bit of tension? Trying to decide, she closed her eyes and debated the choice. What would the spectators want to see?

In her thoughts, she joined them to observe the scene.

What she saw was an exceptionally gorgeous man down on one knee, and a stunning redheaded green-eyed young woman, who by the way, was looking especially slim today, beaming down at him. The imagined picture pleased her. Ever since Steve had made negative comments about one of her friends who'd gained more than a few pounds, she'd become obsessed with her own weight.

She never wanted to hear Steve talk that way about her. Today when she weighed herself, she was elated to see that she was shy of her self-imposed weight limit. She didn't even want to think about what she had to do to stay at that weight. It was only in her dreams that she allowed herself to enjoy a slice of pizza, a pile of mashed potatoes swimming in gravy, or heaven forbid a dish of ice cream. Just the thought of eating forbidden food made her mouth water, but remembering Steve's remark, she swallowed hard. For the thousandth time, she wondered if being just a little bit bulimic would be so terrible. If Steve hadn't been such a great guy in all the other aspects of their relationship, she would have considered moving on.

*****

By one o'clock she was seriously concerned. Steve was never late for anything. Oh, God! Did something bad happen to him? Her heart ached just thinking about how awful it would be to lose him. Standing on her tiptoes, she frantically searched for the sight of him.

Now, not only did she have to pee, she was hungry and her stomach growled just to verify the fact. Ah, she remembered that she'd snatched several pieces of goodies left over from last Halloween and dropped them into her purse.

Voila! Her searching fingers pulled out a rolled-up piece which she eagerly unwrapped and popped into her mouth…only it wasn't candy. It was bubble gum. Even though it tasted wonderful, she had to get rid of it. To be chewing when he asked her The Big Question would ruin the picture-perfect proposal scene.

One ladylike cough sent the gum into her waiting hand where, to her surprise, it turned into instant glue. She'd chewed a lot of bubble gum in her youth and she didn't remember it being so sticky. What if Steve showed up while she was trying with her left hand to pick gum off the hand that he would want to hold while he was proposing to her? Oops! Now her left-hand fingers were stuck together.

Trying to keep a pleasant look on her face, she frantically worked on freeing her hands of the sticky mess while she looked around for a place to get rid of it. There were no public trash receptacles nearby, but there was a large potted plant near the entrance to the restaurant. It wasn't something a good citizen should do, but since she had no other choice, she set her sights on the plant.

Sweet Adeline

Success! With the wad of gum finally rolled into a ball, she was aiming for the plant when she saw him.

He was here!

Chapter 3

Her heart pounded at the sight of her tall, gorgeous and awesome Steve. His blond head was hard to miss because it soared above most of the other walkers. With a warm and exciting smile on her face, she was poised to throw the gum when she noticed a woman who was walking beside him. As they got closer, she could see that he was holding the hand of a tall rather plump but not unattractive female whose frizzy blond hair was bouncing with every step. Addie's eyes widened when she became aware that the woman's hair was not the only thing that was bouncing. Even this far away she could see the material on her red blouse straining to contain the flopping large package underneath.

Addie didn't even realize that her eyes glanced down at her own rather slim chest.

When Steve leaned close to the woman, kissed her cheek, and whispered in her ear, alarm bells rang in Addie's head. A hurried toss sent the gum in the general direction of the plant.

When they finally stood in front of her, Addie didn't say a word; something wasn't right. Where was the hug? Hell, he didn't even look happy to see her. Her foot tapped out an impatient beat on the sidewalk while she waited for him to say something. His eyes were looking everywhere, just not at her. Where was the Steve who'd kissed her so passionately just a few days ago? They'd been together two years on an exclusive basis. The exclusive bit had been his idea right from the beginning, and as far as she knew, they had been.

Steve might not want to look into her eyes, but the woman, whose face appeared altogether too smug to please Addie, had no problem. She had never seen the woman before, and on close inspection the only apparent family resemblance to Steve was her blue eyes; the blond hair didn't count because it could have come out of a bottle. But sometimes even relatives don't share similar features, so this could be Steve's sister, or his niece, or his cousin....

Steve finally spoke. "Addie, I've thought of a dozen ways to tell you this, and none of them were easy. So, I guess I'll just introduce you to Ellen," he paused, glancing down at the woman,

Sweet Adeline

adoration shining on his face, "my wife. We were married yesterday."

All thoughts of dead toes, peeing, and hunger vanished as Addie's world turned black, shutting out his voice that droned on. How could this be? Shaking her head in denial, she tried to remain calm, but her voice betrayed her when she squeaked, "Is this a joke?"

That's when Ellen waved her pudgy hand, flashing the matched ring set.

Addie couldn't believe her eyes. The son-of-a-bitch had bought the set that she'd pointed out as something she found attractive as they'd walked past a jewelry store's display window a few months ago. The bastard had bought the rings, but not for her.

"I'm so sorry, Addie," he said quietly, his eyes downcast. "I thought that you were my soul mate until I ran into Ellen, my high school sweetheart. Addie, I would have been happy with you, but not as happy as I will be with Ellen."

Ellen beamed.

Addie was having trouble breathing. This was not what was supposed to be happening. Where was the Steve who had pledged his undying love just a few days ago?

"But your high school reunion was just last weekend. You figured this out in what? Three days?"

"I know it sounds crazy, but when I saw her again, I knew instantly. When we broke up prom night, my heart was so shattered I flunked my freshman year of college and had to go home." He paused, looked lovingly into Ellen's eyes, and smiled. "My love for Ellen must have been there all along."

Addie swallowed hard, trying to deny her stomach's request to spew her breakfast. Oh, that's right; she hadn't eaten breakfast.

"She was my first love," he continued, "and I guess I never forgot my first love."

Addie stared at him in disbelief. "After two years with me, you changed your mind over a weekend? I can't believe this!"

"Addie. You are such a great person!"

"Cut the crap, Steve. If you dare say 'I hope that we can remain friends,' I'll barf chunks on your shoes."

He looked nervous. "I'd hoped that you wouldn't make a scene."

Too angry to cry, her voice went up the scales while she yelled, "Is that why you had me wait on the sidewalk outside the restaurant? Didn't think I'd make a scene in such a public place? Well, you thought wrong!"

"Addie, please keep your voice down!" he pleaded. "People are watching!"

"Fuck the watchers!" Addie continued to yell. "They want a show? I'll give them a show!"

A spattering of applause from a few of the passing walkers gave her encouragement.

Addie continued at a lower volume, attempting to control her anger, "You said you wanted to ask me something. So far, you've just told me something."

He hung his head. "What I wanted to ask you for was your forgiveness."

That did it. "Forgiveness?" she shrieked. "Forgiveness for what? Forgiveness for taking up two years of my life? How do I get those two years back, Steve? Forgiveness for not giving me a heads-up that you were cheating on me? What, Steve? What is it that I'm supposed to forgive you for?"

She stopped shouting when she noticed that the couple she was yelling at was speed walking away.

Stunned, upset, numb, and angry over Steve's betrayal, she watched the retreating pair in disbelief. How had this happened? Instead of having the expected engagement ring on her finger, she had nothing except the feeling that she'd been run over by a truck.

A momentary respite from her emotional meltdown came when she got a fleeting glimpse of the bottom of Ellen's departing shoe. The big wad of pink bubble gum had found a home.

Chapter 4

Three days following *The Incident*, dawn's ugly light found Addie in bed balled up in the fetal position. Except for necessary trips to the bathroom and snack runs to the kitchen, she hadn't ventured far from her bed. With the covers pulled over her head, she replayed *The Incident* over and over, always hoping for a different ending; no matter how many reruns she watched, the ending was always the same. Steve wasn't hers anymore. How could her heart still be beating when it hurt so badly?

She rolled over, snuggled into the warm covers and was about to go back to sleep when the feeling of guilt jarred her awake. Could it have been her fault? Had she failed Steve in some way that had made him feel free to betray her?

"Enough!" she yelled. Throwing back the covers, she swung her feet onto the floor and stood up. She had done nothing wrong. As if the two years she'd wasted on him weren't enough, realizing that by staying in bed mourning the loss of the back-stabbing-oath-breaking-excuse-for-a-man she had just added three more days.

But it didn't matter how many times she told herself that he wasn't worth it. Her head might believe that, but her heart hadn't gotten the message.

Catching a glimpse of her disheveled appearance in the mirror as she headed for the shower made her flinch. Damn Steve! He wasn't worth it. She needed to go to work because three days were about all she could blame on the stomach flu, her excuse for staying home.

As was her habit every morning, she stepped onto the hated scales while she waited for the hot water to reach the shower. And included in that habit was the ritual of closing her eyes while the scales performed, and then guessing what she would see when she opened them. If the number was higher than her set limit, she panicked. Not wanting Steve's disapproval, she'd diet all day…and then it hit her. She didn't have to please him anymore so it didn't matter what the scales showed. The sense of freedom surprised her.

Upon opening her eyes, she was startled to see that she'd lost more in her three-day mourning period than on any other diet she'd tried. She stood for a moment looking at the number knowing she'd probably never see it again. To stay at that weight she would have to starve herself, and with Steve out of the picture, she didn't have to do that anymore. When her stomach growled, a sudden vision of a high stack of pancakes drowning in syrup danced in her head along with the location of the nearest House of Pancakes.

After a quick shower and dressed in the brightest outfit in her closet, Addie headed out into a Steveless world.

*****

So beautiful was the view, her thoughts of Steve momentarily fled as she drove south along the scenic peninsula road with Lake Michigan on either side of her. The long and narrow finger of land that jutted out into the cold water was the preferred living area for those who worked in the adjacent town. Bikers and joggers were plentiful on the peninsula, and as she drove by one of them, Addie waved; the jogger waved back. Even though she didn't know their names, after seeing them so many times, they felt like friends. Lately there was one new evening jogger, a very pretty but overweight lady whose colorful jacket made her hard to miss.

Within minutes, she reached her destination, parked and entered the House of Pancakes. The smell of sizzling bacon, maple syrup and fried eggs assaulted her nostrils. By the time she was seated at the counter her mouth was watering. When the food that had been off-limits for two years was finally set down in front of her, she savored every bite.

Chapter 5

Addie left the restaurant with a smile on her face and a take-out box under her arm. "Your eyes are bigger than your stomach," her mother used to tell her when she piled too much food on her plate.

She had made it through half of the stack of pancakes when her stomach, unused to heavy food, signaled it was time to stop. It was hard to lay down her fork, but after the waitress offered to box up the rest, she decided that leftover pancakes for lunch sounded pretty good.

There was a spring in her step as she headed for her car to drive to her office a few blocks away. Lifting her head, she felt the warm morning sun on her face, relieved to find that her Steveless world wasn't such a bad place after all.

*****

Pausing at the entrance to her building, Addie took the time to admire the place where she was employed as a writer for the popular magazine, *Your World*. Never in her wildest dreams had she ever pictured herself working for the largest publishing house in the state. The marble foyer, the soaring ceilings, and the glass walls were impressive.

The first time she had entered this building had been for her interview with the magazine's manager, James Lawson.

Her thoughts went back to the day of the interview:

*****

From their initial phone call, she'd pictured him as an older gentleman with years of experience under his belt. Instead, the tall brown-eyed man who stood up to greet her when she entered his office was about her own age. Her eyes were immediately drawn to his thick head of black hair that grew into a peak above his forehead. She'd heard of widow's peaks, but couldn't remember ever seeing one before.

Flustered when she finally noticed that he'd been holding out his hand for her to shake, the folder she had filled with samples of her writing slipped out of her hand and fell to the floor. Papers flew out and fanned themselves across the carpet.

"Oh, how clumsy of me!" she'd exclaimed, her face red with embarrassment.

"No big deal, Miss Parker! Here, let me help you."

When all the papers were back inside the folder and Addie was seated, the interview began.

"We have several openings, Miss Parker, but I see that you're applying for a writing position."

"That's right, Mr. Lawson. Even at a young age, writing came naturally to me. All of my professors at the University urged me to pursue my talent in this field. The papers that you helped me pick up are samples of my writing."

Mr. Lawson nodded and opened the folder to scan a few wrinkled sheets. Addie felt her face flush once again, hoping she hadn't made a complete fool of herself. "Your professors were quite enthusiastic about your writing abilities," Mr. Lawson said, flipping through a few more pages. "But do you have any real writing experience other than your school newspaper and these creative pieces?" he asked.

Addie swallowed.

"Not really, but I have no doubt I'll exceed your expectations," she said, her confidence returning in defense of her skills.

Mr. Lawson sat back in his chair and considered her for a moment before speaking. "There is a writing position open that needs to be filled immediately. Could you start tomorrow?"

She left his office thinking that this was the best moment of her life.

*****

According to the huge clock over the bank of elevators, she'd spent too much time at The House of Pancakes. During the job interview, Mr. Lawson had stressed the importance of being on time; he expected everyone to be at their desks at the stroke of nine o'clock, and not a second later.

Just as she pushed the elevator button, the unfamiliar feeling of a very full stomach suddenly announced that all was not well. What she needed right now was a speedy ride to the bathroom on the sixth floor.

She pushed the button again.

The sound of chattering females made her groan. She absolutely had to disappear into the elevator before they noticed her.

12

Sweet Adeline

The last time she'd ridden the elevator with the ladies from the law firm on the seventh floor, they'd been on their way to lunch. That's when she'd opened her big mouth, and while pointing at her ring finger, hinted that something big was going to happen on her lunch hour. The girls had giggled and hugged her as they all rode the elevator to the ground floor. Flashing the victory sign, she'd blissfully headed for Steve, unaware of the ambush that awaited her.

The ping indicating the arrival of the elevator was music to her ears, but when the door opened and no one seemed in a rush to step out, she started to panic. Two in the front were continuing a conversation, one woman was intent on zipping up her jacket, and from what she could see, it looked as if a couple in the back was making out. Impatiently she tapped her foot and stared hard at the people who were taking their sweet time. Goosebumps that were rising on her arms were being chased away by hot flashes, a clear sign that all was not well.

That's when the guy who had been bent over kissing his girl straightened up. With horror she saw that his blond head soared higher than any of the other passengers.

Steve and Ellen, engrossed in each other, didn't notice Addie until she was in front of them. His sudden intake of breath made it obvious that running into her was the last thing he wanted to do. His edgy, awkward look turned into a phony smile.

"Oh, hello Addie!" he managed to say. "Uh, we just left my lawyer's office on the seventh floor. I was…uh, I was wondering if we'd run into you."

Before she could answer, Ellen hugged his arm while remarking in a possessive sugar-dripping voice, "How nice to see you again! Steve has been telling me such wonderful things about you!"

That was it. Her stomach had run out of patience forcing her to make a choice: her purse or the take-out box.

Addie chose the take-out box.

Steve's gag reflex was so strong that a French kiss could set it off, so what happened next was predictable. Since he didn't have a handy take-out box, when he took off running, his hands were covering his mouth. It gave Addie great joy to wonder where he was depositing his breakfast.

Lifting her eyes off the full-to-the-brim take-out box and by looking through the window, she could see Steve outside hugging

13

the potted plant by the building's entrance. Pedestrians walking by were giving him a wide berth.

Before anyone else could step into the elevator, Addie closed the door and hit the button for the sixth floor.

Chapter 6

Addie stood inside the locked bathroom stall clutching the now-empty take-out box. Maybe flushing the whole disgusting mess at one time hadn't been such a good idea. Holding her breath, she watched in horror as the contents in the backed-up toilet rose to the brim, while the sour stench of vomit clogged the air in the same way the mass was clogging the toilet.

"Stop! Please stop!" she pleaded. When the rising water stopped, Addie slumped against the stall door in relief.

With a few seconds to spare, she was seated at her desk when the second hand on the clock hit twelve. Her mouth might taste sour, her barf-free hair might still be damp, her make-up might be gone, but she wasn't late.

Her computer was just beginning to wake up when she noticed Mr. Lawson heading her way. He was probably coming to congratulate her on the article she'd emailed to him right before she'd left work three days ago. "Wisdom from the Trenches" was the catchy title she had used for the fluff piece she had written, for fluff was what she'd been hired to write. The compensation she received for writing such drivel almost made her forget her dream of becoming a serious author.

"Good morning, Mr. Lawson," she smiled up at him.

Mr. Lawson didn't smile back. In fact, he looked very concerned.

"Miss Parker, are you okay?"

"I'm fine, Mr. Lawson!"

By now he was standing close enough to put his hand on her shoulder. "Are you sure?"

She held her breath. Could he smell her? And why was he touching her? She reached up and tucked her still-damp hair behind her ears. "Really, I'm fine."

Lowering her eyes, she put her finger on the keyboard and started to type. Maybe he'd get the hint that she was busy and move on.

He didn't get the hint.

Evelyn Allen Harper

"You really don't look well, Miss Parker. Could it be that you came back to work too soon? That stomach flu is nasty business."

Trying not to breathe on him, she protested, "No, really, Mr. Lawson! I'm fine."

"But you don't look fine. If you're going to be sick again, I'd prefer that you do it in the restroom and not out here. I insist that you lie down on the couch until you look better."

She could feel the eyes of her fellow workers watching him hovering over her. How embarrassing. Maybe she'd just spend the rest of the day in the bathroom.

It was hard to keep her head high as she made her way past the curious eyes that followed her out of the room. Once in the hall, she ran to the restroom, swung open the door and screamed.

A partially chewed pancake, floating in water that was still streaming down the side of the commode, drifted over her shoe.

Chapter 7

"Everyone listen up," Mr. Lawson announced when he had the attention of the front office workers. "Because of Adeline Parker's quick response yesterday in reporting an overflowing toilet, a potential expensive repair job on the ceiling below on the fifth floor was avoided. Now I understand that we are all are guilty of plugging the toilet once in a while…," and here he had to stop talking to wait for the laughter to die down, "but being good citizens, we report the problem before it has a chance to become a flood. If you have a chance to thank Miss Parker, do it, and if you are the culprit who didn't report that they'd clogged the toilet, then shame on you!"

Addie sat with her head down. To the others, it might look as if she were saying, "Aw, it's no big deal." In reality, her head was hanging because she was realizing how easy it was going to be to figure out the culprit. After all, it was the ladies' bathroom, and that eliminated more than half of the people in the front office. Asking the women what they'd eaten for their last meal would solve the mystery. At least it would if everyone told the truth which she had no intention of doing. Since she had repeated Steve's aversion of fat women to a few of her fellow workers, office gossip would have spread the word; no one would even consider that she was the one who'd eaten pancakes.

Now why did she have to go and think of that betraying-low-down-son-of-a-bitch? It was hard enough to keep him out of her thoughts without inviting him with just a casual observance. Well, he *had* been her whole life for two years. Her head might try to shut him out, but her heart wasn't cooperating because it was still trying to recover from the big aching hole in it. He'd made the fat statement only once, but she never forgot that he had said it.

Turning back to her computer, she was startled to find an instant message from Mr. Lawson. Could it be that he'd seen from her brilliant writing in the "Wisdom from the Trenches" article that she was capable of so much more than just fluff pieces?

Lawson – Please see me when you get a chance.

Mr. Lawson looked up from what looked like a financial report.

"Have a seat, Miss Parker."

The concerned look on his face alarmed her. Rather than the face of a man who was going to praise her for a well-written article, it was the face of a man who was going to fire her. She needed this job. How else could she pay her rent, buy food, make car payments, pay utilities and her student loans? Perched on the edge of her chair, she kept repeating to herself, "Don't cry, don't cry, don't cry."

He sighed, laid down the sheet of paper and opened his mouth.

Addie briefly closed her eyes and her ears to help deaden the blow. "….and so, Miss Parker, how does that sound to you?"

Her eyes flew open. He hadn't fired her! But what was he talking about?

"Mr. Lawson, would you please repeat that?"

"I said *Your World* is in trouble. We are just a few issues short of going under. The numbers aren't good."

"No, after that. What did you say after that?"

"Perhaps you shouldn't have closed your eyes while I was talking to you. Miss Parker, it looked as if you thought I was going to bite you."

Should she admit it? "Mr. Lawson, I thought…well, the paper, with all those figures were troubling you, and well, I th…th...thought…."

"You thought what, Miss Parker?"

"I thought you were going to fire me." The words flew out of her mouth in a rush of air.

He took a moment to observe the very beautiful but much too thin woman who was looking at him with troubled green eyes. "That might happen down the road a bit, but not right now."

"Down the road?" Anxiety knocked the wind out of her lungs. Her eyes glazed over as once again figures ran through her head; rent, food, car payment, utilities, and student loans. How was she going to survive if she lost her job? "How far down the road?"

"How far down the road depends on the people who work here. To save *Your World*, future articles have to be sharper, the subjects more interesting, and the pictures have to be more captivating. In other words, *Your World* has to be a better magazine than our competition. Either that, or we fold."

Sweet Adeline

Fold? That would mean no job…don't go there. It was a relief that her job wasn't in immediate jeopardy. Her heart felt lighter when, in a normal voice, she asked, "Have you talked to the others?"

"Not yet, but I will. Since your article gave me an idea, I thought I'd start with you."

She knew it! Finally, he was going to give her a serious assignment. No more fluff articles on how to send your child to school with a nutritious lunch that he wouldn't trade or throw into the trash. Or how about the one on how to pick the right napkin and centerpiece to bring out the colors in your china? That one about did her in.

She smiled, raised her eyebrows, and asked shyly, "Does that mean that you liked "Wisdom from the Trenches"?"

Mr. Lawson never openly praised anyone's work. The only sign that he tolerated any of it was the check that he handed out on payday.

"I didn't say I liked it, Miss Parker. I said it gave me an idea."

"Oh."

"In your article, you presented some very interesting stories about people who had problems. It wasn't the problems that got my attention but the caustic off-the-cuff-tongue-in-cheek replies. If I like it, there's a good chance our readers will, too."

"Oh."

"Miss Parker, is that all you can say?"

"I don't know what else to say," Addie was puzzled. Whatever he'd said while she was concentrating on not crying must have been important.

With a relieved smile on his face, he beamed, "Does that mean you'll do it?"

"Do what?"

"Oh, for heaven's sake! Weren't you listening to anything?"

Addie's face turned a shade pinker than her lip-gloss. "I apologize, Mr. Lawson. It won't happen again."

"It better not," he barked. "I said I wasn't going to fire you, but I could change my mind!"

"No, no," Addie shook her head. "Please don't say that! It's just that the thought of losing my job makes me a little crazy. Just give me another chance, Mr. Lawson. What did you ask me to do?"

Chapter 8

Addie made her way back to her desk on autopilot, bumping into desks and ignoring the greetings of her coworkers. She didn't know whether she should be laughing right now because he hadn't fired her, or crying right now because of what he'd ask her to do so that she wouldn't be fired in the near future.

It was all because of that dumb article she'd written. Mr. Lawson had finally complimented her, and that was good, but it had given him an idea, and that was bad.

He wanted her to write an anonymous advice column that even her coworkers wouldn't know she was writing. Since she wouldn't be producing anything specific for the magazine that they would see, the story would be that he had assigned her some special research project that was taking up all her time.

She looked at her hands and wiggled the fingers that were supposed to be writing the great American novel. Instead, those fingers were going to produce more drivel. And the name she was going to write under? Dr. Ask-Me-Anything.

*****

Mr. Lawson's underlying threat of "Screw this up and you're out of here," hung in the air as Addie held her head in her hands and reread what her boss had written as a pretend advice request. Addie viewed the exercise as a test.

Dear Dr. Ask-Me-Anything,

I sure hope you can help me. Me and my husband are newlyweds but don't worry, I won't be asking for any advice about sex because I don't need it since sex has been good ever since our first date. The problem is that he don't like my cooking. He wants to bring his widowed mother to live with us so that she can do it. I admit that I ain't a very good cooker. Should I let him do this?

Lonely in the Kitchen

Addie took a deep breath, and typed.

Dear Lonely,

Sweet Adeline

What makes you think I give a shit about your problem?
Quit bothering me and figure it out for yourself.

Dear Lonely,
Sounds like you were born stupid and had a relapse. Did
you pick this clown out all by yourself? Once Mother gets a
foothold in your house, watch out! She'll be in your bedroom next.
Hey, have you thought of taking cooking lessons? Get a spine, lady.

She sat back and read her response. Did her fingers actually
type those words? *Come on*, she told herself, *your job is on the line!
Remember rent, food, car payment…*

Dear Lonely,
Hey, Lady! Buy a cookbook, for heaven's sake! Cooking
ain't rocket science!

Dear Lonely,
You know that thing that runs down your back? It's called a
backbone. Use it, unless having your mother-in-law in the next
bedroom listening to you and your husband playing hide the wiener
turns you on.

Her fingers stopped typing. Coffee. Maybe a cup would
make the job of writing trash easier.
After a quick trip to the kitchen for a caffeine fix, she soon
was back at her computer, her fingers poised above the keyboard.

Dear Lonely,
Lady, God gave you brains to figure out things like this.
Find someone who gives a crap and ask them because I sure don't.

Her hands dropped into her lap. How far those fingers had
fallen. Her university professors would cringe if they knew their
prized student was writing such nonsense.

Dear Lonely,
Whoa! Nip this idea in the bud! Two cooks will spoil your
marriage along with the broth.

Evelyn Allen Harper

Dear Lonely,

Her fingers paused, waiting for inspiration that refused to show its face. She typed….Blah, blah, blah, stupid idea, blah, blah, blah, #$@&%*! Mother-in-law, blah, blah, blah advice….

Just how 'Send' got involved in her misery was never explained, but it happened. Like magic, her trial replies appeared on Mr. Lawson's computer.

Chapter 9

Addie covered her face with her hands. Now, she'd done it. The samples that Mr. Lawson were not meant to see were now on his computer. She couldn't imagine his reaction when he read them. If she couldn't convince him that she was just venting her displeasure at being given another fluff assignment, her road to unemployment had just been shortened.

The sound of someone clearing his throat startled her. If she lowered her hands, whoever it was would see how upset she was. "Go away," she whispered. "Just leave me alone."

The sensation of something soft brushed across her hands.

"It's a tissue. Take it, Miss Parker."

Oh, no! That was Mr. Lawson's voice.

"Meet me in my office."

Using the tissue, she wiped her eyes, blew her nose, and headed for his office with "dead woman walking" running through her head.

Mr. Lawson looked up from his computer. "Miss Parker, I can see you're upset. Did you get bad news? Do you need to leave early today?"

She didn't trust her voice, so she just shook her head.

"Boyfriend problems?"

What was going on? Why all this concern when he was just going to fire her anyhow? She closed her eyes and waited for the blow.

"Hey, no boyfriend is worth it. Maybe when you tell him that you just got your own office he'll wish he'd treated you better."

Her eyes flew open.

"It's not a corner office and it doesn't have a window, but it's a start. If your column takes off like I think it will, who knows where you'll end up?"

She was speechless.

He smiled. "You weren't expecting this?"

She took a deep breath. "I thought you were going to fire me because you didn't like my sample replies."

"Not like them? I'm sure with a little practice you'll get better, but with the exception of that last one, I loved them!"

"Whew!" she exclaimed and without asking permission, flopped down on a chair. "What a relief! I was just making up fun replies and sending them to you was an accident."

"You thought I wouldn't like them and fire you?"

She nodded.

"Well, worry no more! Clean out your desk and follow me."

Chapter 10

"…and then, do you know what that bitch said to me? No, no, don't even try. It's too awful to repeat, but I'll tell you this, the next time that fake-blond-excuse-for-a-secretary pushes ahead of me in the cafeteria line, she'll find herself on the floor looking up at the ceiling." Ellen paused to grab a breath. "Have I told you about the food in that cafeteria? They know we're captive because how far can you go for lunch when you just have forty-five minutes? It's awful! Well, I suppose I could pack a lunch, but you know how rushed our mornings are, Honey. I suppose we could start our morning love fest a bit earlier," she paused to give Steve a wink, "but why mess with a routine that's perfect?"

Out of the corner of his eye, Steve was watching Ellen's mouth moving. Was she ever going to shut up? He had no memory of her non-stop chatter during their high school courtship.

"Don't you think that's right?"

"Wh…what?" Steve stuttered.

"Don't tell me you weren't listening! Aren't you interested in my thoughts?" Ellen's face puckered up.

He reached over and patted her hand. "I was listening, Baby! I just got distracted by a car that pulled out in front of us."

"I didn't see a car pull out in front of us. What are you talking about?"

"Yes, there was one. You just didn't see it."

"Now you're telling me I'm not seeing things?"

"Let it go, Honey. The traffic is heavy tonight and I'm driving extra careful because I have my precious Ellen in the car."

"Oh, that's so sweet!" She reached over, grabbed his hand off the wheel and kissed it. "I haven't even gotten to the best part of the story."

"Uh, there's a story?"

"Yes! Don't you remember? I was talking about lunch time in the cafeteria."

"Oh, now I remember. So what happened in the cafeteria?"

"Well, you remember the guy two cubicles down from mine? The one with the scraggy mustache and the paunch? Him and his girlfriend, who is nothing to write home about but that's another story, were making meth in their bathtub! They live in a large apartment complex. They could have blown up the whole building! That's what everyone was talking about at lunch today. Can you believe they were stupid enough to do something like that? I guess they were making a lot of money, but how can you spend money when you're in prison? Some people just don't have the brains God gave a bird! Are we stopping to eat? I'm too tired to cook. All I want to do is sit in a quiet booth so that we can talk while we eat our meal."

Steve could feel his exasperation reaching the explosive level. Would running into a telephone pole shut her up?

Chapter 11

Steve sat at his desk and tried to look as if the long phone conversation was work-related. This was Ellen's third call of the day, and if today was anything like previous days, there would be three more calls before closing time. Holding the phone away from his ear didn't help and it didn't change anything. Steve had no problem hearing Ellen's rambling account of what had happened at lunch with the meth couple.

"…and do you believe they weren't embarrassed? Well, if they were, it sure didn't look like it. I guess they're out on bail right now, but they're facing serious prison time when they see the judge next week…."

Steve zoned out.

"…and then I said to him, 'Lookit, fellow, you can't talk to me that way! My husband is going to be very upset with you when I tell him what you called me.'" Ellen paused in her rant breathing heavily, waiting for a response. "Uh, Steve? You are upset, aren't you? Steve? Are you there? Have you been listening to me?"

He jerked himself back to the present. "Of course I've been listening, Honey! And you know I am upset when someone mistreats my wife. But can we end this call? Work is piling up on my desk and if you want me home in time for dinner, I need to get back to work."

"Oh, Steve, just thinking about seeing you sitting at the table eating dinner with me gives me goosebumps."

Ellen was trying, but some of her cooking efforts left a lot to be desired. The thought of eating another meal that consisted of overcooked meat and undercooked vegetables was enough for Steve to say, "You've worked all day, Honey. Instead of eating at home, why don't we meet at Joe's Bar and Grill for dinner?"

"Oh, Steve! Yes! And can we pretend it's a date? We got married so fast we really didn't have time to go through the courtship stage." She giggled. "I might even mess with you under the table."

Steve flinched. "Ah, gotta go. See you at Joe's at six."

"I love you so much! I'm hanging up right now because I don't want you to be late. Love ya! Bye."

He hung up the phone, laid his forehead on the desk and muttered, "Dear God, what have I gotten myself into?"

*****

Steve and Ellen were sitting at a table at Joe's Bar and Grill, holding hands and looking into each other's eyes. There was soft music in the background for those who could hear it, but Steve couldn't. Ellen was recounting one of their high-school memories in a loud voice and effectively blocking out everything else. She might have been looking into his eyes with love, but he was looking into her eyes attempting to send her a mental command to shut up.

His hope of a quiet dinner fled when the food finally arrived and he discovered that his bride could talk and chew at the same time. They'd dated just for the last semester of their senior year of high school. How many memories could they have made in just twelve weeks? Apparently, a lot and Ellen remembered them all.

"…and then do you remember what Mr. Marsh said when he found out that I wasn't really in his class but was there to be with you? You don't? Well, I do! It was funny and everyone laughed, not like the time when we got caught under the bleachers making out and got hauled into the principal's office. I was so afraid they were going to call our parents, but thank God they didn't…."

Steve closed his ears and ate. They were on the dessert course when things changed.

"….and that's when I remembered what you said that night when we talked about how it would be when we were married. You said that you wanted kids right away, and that no wife of yours would ever work outside the house because you wanted her to be there with a hot dinner on the table when you came home from work. So, I'm glad we are having this dinner tonight, kind of a celebration, because I gave notice today at work and I quit taking the pill right after we got married so I could even be pregnant right now."

The 'p' word opened his ears.

"What?" Steve's eyes were wild. "What did you just say?"

Ellen's ice cream loaded spoon paused on its way to her mouth. "There you go again. You weren't listening. I'm beginning to believe you don't like to hear my thoughts."

"Ellen, please. Just repeat the last thing that you said."

Sweet Adeline

Ellen pouted, "You mean the part where I said that I'm leaving my job or the part about not taking the pill?"

Steve's world crumbled.

*****

It was the cold breeze coming in from the open curtainless window that woke Steve. Goosebumps and chattering teeth made him search for the covers that seemed to be, once again, missing from his side of the bed. Enough light was coming in from the open window for Steve to see that the rather large lump beside him was wrapped like a mummy, head included. Ellen was the one who'd insisted that she couldn't sleep without fresh air and Steve, who just wanted to be a good husband, had gone along with her.

Since the idea of unraveling the mummy in his frozen state was not inviting, thoughts of a hot shower propelled him out of his cold bed.

With closed eyes, Steve stood under the hot spray that was doing a good job of chasing away the goosebumps. That's when two things happened. The first thing was that the curtain parted and Ellen stepped in. The second thing was that he found himself wishing the hot spray could get rid of more than just goosebumps.

"Need your back scrubbed?" Ellen giggled as her hands searched and grabbed.

"That's not my back," Steve managed to gasp before he leaned his head back and closed his eyes.

Ellen kept on talking while her hands remained busy. "I just had to get out of that warm bed! I was sweating! And why do you have the water so hot? Here, I'll just make it right for you." One of her busy hands stopped long enough to reach out and change the water setting. "There. Now isn't that better? Just stick with me, Sweetie, Mama will take good care of you!"

His eyes flew open as the cool water hit.

"Uh, the thought was nice, but I'm not interested," he said quietly as he pushed her away and stepped out of the shower.

Ellen stood alone under the cool water spray. "Steve?" she called, wondering what she'd done wrong.

Chapter 12

Jeb Linden tried to hide his puffing-out-of-shape body behind a skinny tree. So far, it hadn't been easy but he'd succeeded in staying out of sight of his jogging wife. She was up to something, but what? Whatever it was, it had started two weeks ago around dinnertime. Her nervous sneak-peeks at the kitchen clock got his attention to begin with, but when Cindy, a woman who hated exercise, decided that jogging after the evening meal was a good thing, he became suspicious.

Was she meeting someone? He waited until she'd turned the corner before venturing out of his cover, unaware that the scowling owner of the tree was bearing down on him, a water hose in his hand and malice in his eyes.

"Take that, you pervert!" the man yelled as he turned on the water, hitting Jeb in the back with a cold stream.

"Yipes!" Jeb yelled. He turned and confronted the man. "What the hell do you think you're doing?"

"Hanging around here, trying to sneak a peek at my wife, are you? If I see you on my property again, I'll have something other than a water hose in my hand. Now get out of here before I call the cops!"

"I wasn't sneaking a peek at anyone, you idiot!"

"Ha," the man sneered and hit him with another blast. "Who's the idiot? You're the one who's soaking wet."

Jeb held up his dripping wet arms to indicate surrender and headed home.

When Cindy returned from her jog an hour and a half later, he was watching the evening news.

"Did you have a good run?" he asked.

"Sure did!" she replied.

"See anyone interesting?"

She stopped in her tracks. "Like who?"

"I don't know. Another jogger, maybe?"

"No, I didn't. Oh, one of the neighbors was watering his lawn with a hose. I was going to say 'Hi' to him, but he didn't look

Sweet Adeline

friendly." She headed for the stairs. "I'm going to take a shower now."

He watched Cindy until she was out of sight. Was his wife cheating on him?

*****

Morning came too early for Jeb who had been awake most of the night watching his sleeping wife. The thought of her even hugging another man made this heart hurt. As far as he was concerned, their marriage was almost perfect, but did Cindy feel that way? It was the fear of hearing that she was unhappy that kept him from waking her. For right now, ignorance was bliss.

If Cindy were cheating on him, she was hiding it quite well. There was nothing different in their conversation over breakfast or their goodbye kiss as he dropped her off at work. Either she was a good actress or what she was doing wasn't hurting her conscience, and to him, that was worse than just cheating.

His old car coughed and rattled as he continued on to where he worked at the lumberyard. Putting off getting the car fixed wasn't going to work anymore. Not having it for a few days would be inconvenient and traveling by taxi to work and back was going to be expensive. It was a wreck of a car, but it was better than no car at all.

He made it through the day on autopilot. All he could think about was Cindy. Trying to imagine life without her was hard to even think about.

*****

Dinner that night was a bucket of chicken from the Colonel. Not only did his wife remove the crunchy coating off the chicken, she also hadn't touched the mashed potatoes and gravy. The light went on in Jeb's head when he connected her changed eating habits with her new physical activity. She was trying to lose weight! Looking at Cindy with a critical eye, he had to admit that she no longer could be called petite. His hand found its way to his own soft stomach and pinched. The two of them had fit so well together, the added pounds had just snuck up on them. But why hadn't she mentioned that she wanted to get back into shape?

Of course! She wasn't on a diet to please him. She was on a diet to please another man. Bile crept up his throat.

"Bye, honey!" Cindy called as the door slammed shut behind her.

Jeb waited for her to turn the corner of the block before he followed her. After a few minutes, he was huffing and puffing and looking around for a place to stop and catch his breath. Jogging was not for sissies. Finding shade under a tree, he was preparing to sit down when the sound of deep breathing alerted him. He was not alone.

Teeth grabbed the back of his jacket and held on. He couldn't turn around to see, but he could hear the growl of what had to be a large dog.

"Good dog!" Jeb yelled.

"Go home!"

"Heel!" Jeb commanded, desperation making his voice crack.

"Help!" he shouted.

The more Jeb yelled, the harder the dog pulled. Desperate, Jeb gave up the fight, struggled out of his jacket, and ran for his life. He didn't even want to think of what Cindy was going to say about his losing one of their matching jackets.

While he was waiting for his wife to return, he picked up *Your World*, the magazine she had gotten in today's mail. Leafing through it, he stopped when he came to the article about a Dr. Ask-Me-Anything who was promising to advise readers on any subject they wished. Did "any subject" include asking for advice on how to handle the problem of a cheating wife?

With no one else to go to for help, Jeb searched through Cindy's desk looking for paper, pen and an envelope. Before he could talk himself out of doing such an out-of-character act, he wrote it, sealed the envelope, walked to the next block where there was a mailbox and dropped in his plea for help.

Chapter 13

Waiting for the response to the new Dr. Ask-Me-Anything notice her boss had put into the last issue of *Your World*, Addie sat in her own office and tried to look busy. The word had spread that she had been assigned a project that required a lot of research. Aside from envying her the private office, most of her coworkers were thankful it was Addie who had been chosen to work with their tough manager.

She was in the middle of yet another game of solitaire when her boss entered her office, shut the door behind him, and threw an envelope on her desk.

"Here we go! I was hoping for a lot more than this, but it's a start."

Knowing that her job would be hanging on what she would write in the form of advice to the request, she didn't pick it up.

"I know I made you think that keeping your job depends on the success of this new little venture of ours, but it's not," he remarked as he reached for the envelope. "You are a talented writer and I'd be a fool to let you go."

Her eyes widened. This was a side of Mr. Lawson that she hadn't seen.

He opened the envelope, cleared his throat, and read:

Dear Dr. Ask-Me-Anything,

I think my wife is cheating on me but I'm afraid to ask her. She hates exercise, but she's taken up jogging and I notice she's not eating carbs. I've been trying to follow her when she jogs, but I'm too out of shape to keep her in sight.

I can't sleep. I can't eat. My heart is breaking. I can't stand the thought of another man touching her.

What should I do?

I'm going crazy! Please, please! Help me!

Worried in the Suburbs

*****

"Make me proud. Just remember, your replies are supposed to be caustic and sarcastic." Mr. Lawson laid the letter back on Addie's desk and walked out of her office.

She sat for a few minutes, her fingers poised over her computer's keyboard, trying to find the words that would make her boss's new venture successful.

Dear Worried in the Suburbs,
When did you first notice that you'd turned into a wimpy little girl? Come on, Worried, grow some balls!
Face the problem head on. Ask her for heaven's sake! Ignorance is not bliss. It's stupid.
Oh, by the way, keep jogging.
Dr. Ask-Me-Anything

Dear Worried in the Suburbs,
Is your wife bigger than you? Can she bench-press more weight than you can? Does she always win when your fights become physical? Is that why you're afraid to ask her if she's having an affair?
If the answers to the above questions are yes, then asking her might get you injured. You have to decide if it's worth a little pain to find out.
I'm sure there's a nurse in the hospital who will help you mail me your next request.
Keep jogging.
Dr. Ask-Me-Anything

Dear Worried in the Suburbs,
You know that thing that runs down the middle of your back? It's called a spine.
Not knowing is not going to change what your wife is doing, so man-up and ask her.
Keep jogging. Sounds like you need it.
Dr. Ask-Me-Anything

Dear Worried in the Suburbs,
Are you and your wife on speaking terms? If you are, the next time the two of you are talking about anything, just slip in, "Are you having an affair?" A little practice will help. "What are we

Sweet Adeline

having for dinner and are you having an affair?" Or, "I like your new hair style and are you having an affair?" Get it?

Let me know how it works out.

Oh, yes. Keep jogging.

Dr. Ask-Me-Anything

Dear Worried in the Suburbs,
Tell me, do you pee sitting down?
Dear Worried in the Suburbs,
Pull up your big-boy pants and act like a man!

Dear Worried in the Suburbs....

Addie laid her forehead on the top of her computer closed her eyes and sighed. This request had not come from a frat guy; it was a real cry for help. Rereading her replies, she realized she couldn't use any of them. Worried deserved a real answer.

Chapter 14

Crossing his arms around himself, Steve tried to silence the rumbling sounds coming from his empty stomach. It was near the end of the lunch hour and he was trying to look casual while waiting for Addie to come out of the restaurant across the street. He refused to think of himself as a stalker. All he wanted was one glimpse of her—just one glimpse. The crushing regret that was consuming his soul hovered over him like a black cloud. How could he have been so stupid? He had traded the real thing that he had with Addie for an adolescent high school crush with Ellen who he didn't even like anymore. Unable to eat or sleep, he bumbled his way through the day missing deadlines and important appointments. Already he was getting curious looks from his coworkers, and he knew eventually he was going to be called into the front office. When that happened, what was he going to say in his defense? Did he even have a defense? Does, "I married the wrong woman," count?

Steve held his breath as the door of the restaurant opened. Not wanting her to see him, he stepped behind a parked car and tried to stay out of sight, which was more difficult to do than he had initially thought; his height and blond hair made it hard to stay unnoticed.

Ah, there she was, the real love that he had thrown away with such disregard. When the sun chose that moment to peek through the clouds and bathe her in golden light, he couldn't stand it any longer. His mouth went dry and his heart skipped a beat as he rounded the parked car and stepped off the curb. Feeling frantic, his brain was trying to think of a surprised greeting that didn't sound made-up when what he saw froze his feet in the middle of the street.

Addie wasn't alone. In fact, she was looking back over her shoulder at a tall well-built man who was following her. He must have said something funny because when she turned her head around, he could see her laughing face. But it was when the man threw his arm around her shoulder as they walked away that made Steve's legs refuse to move. Honking horns and screeching brakes brought him back to reality.

*****

Sweet Adeline

One look at Addie's questioning face told Jim Lawson that throwing his arm around her shoulder was probably not the wisest thing to do. He allowed himself one brief squeeze before he dropped his arm.

His attraction to her, which had started during the hiring interview, had steadily grown over time into the closest thing to love that Jim had ever experienced. Since she had never hesitated to mention her steady boyfriend, he had suffered quietly in the background while nursing a bruised heart. Even though he knew it was wrong, sometimes he even found reasons to criticize her work just to make her notice him. Putting her in charge of the new Dr. Ask-Me-Anything addition to the magazine was sheer brilliance on his part. The excuse for lunch today was to talk about it.

As they walked, he continued their discussion about the next issue of *Your World*.

"Addie, since the issue will be carrying the first Dr. Ask-Me-Anything letter, I'd like to ask you a question about your reply to Worried in the Suburbs."

She stopped walking. "I was wondering when you'd get around to that."

"I thought I'd made it plain that the new feature wasn't a real advice column but just a way to entertain our readers with caustic tongue-in-cheek replies. Was there a reason that there was none of that in your reply to Worried?"

She turned her head to answer her boss who was behind her. "Mr. Law...Jim...I tried. I really did. In fact, I wrote several pretty cynical ones. But Worried sounded like a truly nice man who loved his wife and thought Dr. Ask-Me-Anything could help him. When it came time to submit the letter for publication, my fingers just wouldn't type those caustic words."

Jim threw back his head and laughed. "Addie, you are wonderful! I'm proud that I have a writer who has magic fingers."

Their laughter was drowned out by shrieking brakes and honking horns. By the time Addie whirled around to see what was causing the problem, traffic was moving smoothly.

The two of them exited the elevator on the sixth floor and Addie, unaware of Mr. Lawson's feelings, thanked him for lunch and shut herself in her office.

It had felt strange seeing a face other than Steve's across the table. For two years, lunch together had been the highlight of their day. It was hard for her to believe that the guy who claimed he loved her had found it so easy to walk away from her. Had he always been so lacking in character and she just hadn't seen it? She shook her head. There was no point in trying to understand it all now. Steve was a married man and no matter how much she missed him, she just had to let him go.

Chapter 15

Jeb shivered. He'd spent too much time looking for his jacket and now he could see that Cindy was so far ahead of him he'd never catch up. He'd even looked for Cindy's identical bright-colored jacket but he couldn't find hers either. It didn't help his mood when he finally remembered what had happened to his; the dog had it. By now, it was probably chewed to pieces.

He was too cold just to walk home, so he lengthened his stride and broke into a trot. Having to admit that it felt good to move his body was too much for the inactive Jeb to admit, so he told himself that he was just jogging to keep warm.

Maybe the next issue of his wife's favorite magazine would be in today's mail. Just the thought of how Dr. Ask-Me-Anything would advise him put an extra push into his stride. He had never done anything like that before, but then he had never had a possible cheating wife before. Anyhow, no one would ever know that he was the one asking for advice.

Sure enough, when he checked the mailbox at the end of the driveway, the magazine along with some bills had been delivered earlier that day. Jeb grabbed the magazine, found the Dr. Ask-Me-Anything section, and searched for his question and the doctor's reply. He was surprised that his was the only inquiry. When his eyes landed on his letter, he couldn't help but smile. He'd been published!

*****

Dear Dr. Ask-Me-Anything,

I think my wife is cheating on me but I'm afraid to ask her. She hates exercise, but she's taken up jogging and I notice she's not eating carbs. I've been trying to follow her when she jogs, but I'm too out of shape to keep her in sight.

I can't sleep. I can't eat. My heart is breaking. I can't stand the thought of another man touching her.

What should I do?

I'm going crazy! Please, please! Help me!

Worried in the Suburbs

*****

Evelyn Allen Harper

Dear Worried,

You sound like a nice guy who loves his wife and doesn't want to ruin what you think is a good marriage by confronting her. You need to know that being suspicious of her every move will destroy your marriage as effectually as the affair that you think she's having.

Ignorance is not bliss. In this case, it's stupid.

My advice to you is in two parts.

Following your wife is creepy, so stop it.

The second is to confront her, and then be man enough to face the consequence.

Good luck.

Dr. Ask-Me-Anything

*****

Jeb sat with *Your World* in his hand and read the response several times. Dare he ask his wife? What if her truthful answer shattered their marriage? Maybe if he waited just a few weeks, even a month or two, the novelty of her new love would burn out and then he could pretend it had never happened.

His eyes fell back on Dr. Ask-Me-Anything's reply. Was he man enough to face the end result if Cindy admitted that she was cheating on him? He shook his head, trying to remove an image of her smiling at another man. Had he failed her in some way? She knew he loved her, although he had to admit that he hadn't actually put it into words recently, but then neither had she.

Needing air, he grabbed a sweater and headed out the door. If he walked in the area where Cindy liked to jog, maybe they'd cross paths. Better yet, maybe he'd see what she was up to. Wouldn't she be surprised!

His thoughts went back to how it all started. Remembering the shocked looks on the faces of the drama club members the day he showed up to audition for a part in the next play, he chuckled. He was broke and needed money, and the bet wasn't that he had to get the part, he just had to go through the humiliation of auditioning for it.

Big, muscular and clumsy, he looked out of place and almost walked out when he found out the play was a musical and he'd have to sing. Had his football buddies known it was a musical? Is that why they laughed so hard when he'd accepted the bet?

Sweet Adeline

The reading part of the audition was easy, especially when he found that his love interest in the play would be Cindy, a pretty little thing who he'd never noticed before. When he found out later that she'd been in many of his classes, he was pleasantly surprised.

Vile thoughts rushed through his head about what he was going to do to his buddies when it came time for him to prove that he could sing.

"What have you prepared to sing for us?" he was asked.

His mouth went dry. "Prepared?"

"Well, yes. We need to hear you sing."

He shook his head and was turning to leave when someone suggested, "How about a song that everyone knows? Could you sing Happy Birthday for us?"

What was one more humiliation? Taking a deep breath, he sang the song in a voice that was as big as he was.

He got the part.

It was during the dance scene when he and Cindy sang to each other that the wonderful thing happened; they fell in love.

The day after high-school graduation, they got married and lived happily ever after. Or so he'd thought. Evidently Cindy hadn't.

*****

Jeb slowed down his walk when he felt a headache coming on. Disappointed that he hadn't run into Cindy, he headed for home. The walk had been good, but it hadn't solved any of his problems.

Jeb opened the door to an empty house. Imagining what Cindy was doing right now was making his head pound. Two aspirins and a mouthful of water later, he stretched out on the couch.

The first thing he noticed when he next opened his eyes was that his headache was gone. The second thing he noticed was that the room was dark. Cindy must have gotten home, and seeing him asleep on the couch, hadn't bothered to wake him.

"Cindy?" he called. When there was no answer he called out again, "Cindy, are you home?"

He pushed himself off the couch, turned on the lights and looked at the clock on the wall. He scratched his head and went upstairs to check their bedroom; maybe she had gone straight to bed. "Cindy?" he whisper-yelled into their room, squinting into the dark. When there was no response he flicked on the light but she wasn't there.

"Cindy? Where are you?" he called as he ran from room to room. It took him two passes through the empty house to convince himself that his wife wasn't there. What was he to do now? Go out and trace her jogging route to see if maybe she had fallen or twisted her ankle, or…

*****

The doorbell's ring startled him. Cindy always took her house key when she jogged, so why was she ringing the bell? Or maybe it wasn't Cindy. The guy at the garage had promised to drop off their car yesterday and hadn't called to explain why he never showed up. Jeb had a few choice words to say to the guy. But if it were Cindy ringing the bell, what had she been doing all this time? The black suspicion that reared its ugly head made him feel strong enough to accept the outcome of a confrontation with her.

His decision made, he eagerly opened the door feeling more than ready to tackle either Cindy or the mechanic, and found himself looking into the eyes of a uniformed officer-of-the-law.

"Mr. Jeb Linden?" the officer asked.

Jeb managed to nod his head. Swallowing hard, he replied, "Yeah, that's me. Can I help you?"

Flashing his badge, the policeman identified himself. "I'm Sergeant Joe Green. Are you the husband of Cindy Linden?"

The seed of fear that had been planted when he first saw the cop on his doorstep suddenly had a growth spurt. "Yes, I am. I've been waiting for her to get back from her evening jog. She's never been this late before."

"May I come in?"

"Wait a minute!" Jeb felt the fear factor take over. His heart was pounding, his mouth was dry, and his voice shook when he demanded, "What's going on?"

Sergeant Green stepped past Jeb and entered the house. "To begin with, have you left your home in the past few hours?"

"Why yes, I have. I took a short walk, but for the rest of the time I was right here. I had a headache and took some aspirin. Guess I fell asleep on the couch."

"Do you have any witnesses who will back up your story?"

Jeb frowned, trying to remember. "No, I didn't see anyone on my walk.

"And you were all alone in this house the rest of the time?"

Sweet Adeline

"Just Cindy and I live here and she's out jogging, so yes, I was all alone. What's this about?"

The officer grimaced and flipped his note pad closed.

It was then that a terrible feeling settled in Jeb's stomach. Life as he knew it was about to change. The cop's lips were moving, but whatever he was saying was being drowned out by his pounding heart. Something bad had happened to Cindy. Had she been hit by a car? His knees turned to water.

Sgt. Green became alarmed when Jeb lost his balance and stumbled.

"Mr. Linden, please sit down. Do you need some water?"

Jeb backed up to a chair and collapsed. Whatever Sgt. Green had said, he hadn't heard, but he knew it was bad.

Jeb shook his head. "No, but I do need you to repeat what you just said. I'm sorry, but I just blacked out there for a second. Was Cindy in an accident? Is she hurt?"

"Your wife is dead, Mr. Linden."

Jeb gave a startled sob. "Dead? My Cindy is dead? You've got to be mistaken! M…m…my Cindy, she can't, she can't be dead," he cried through clenched teeth, his voice softening as each word echoed throughout the empty house. "You're wrong, you have to be!"

Sgt. Green cleared his throat; he hated this part of his job. "I'm sorry, Mr. Linden. Her body was found behind the hedge on your neighbor's property. She'd been hit on the head from behind and dragged to where she was found. It was a hard blow," he paused before he added, "There was no pain; she died instantly."

Jeb collapsed.

Chapter 16

It had been days since he'd had his last glimpse of Addie. Steve thought he knew her routine as well as his own, but for some reason, she wasn't showing up at the regular places. Getting desperate, he had become bold in his stalking, not taking as much care to not be seen. In the end, it hadn't mattered because she never appeared.

Trying to ignore subtle hints that were coming from the front office, he pretended that everything at work was all right as day after day he disappeared for an hour.

Realizing that he'd been away too long, he was about to turn around and head back when he noticed that he had company. Alarms went off in his head when he found himself sandwiched between two uniformed policemen.

To Steve, it seemed impossible that in the blink of an eye he'd been handcuffed, taken to jail and accused of murdering someone he didn't know.

Who could he call? The officers probably wouldn't believe his story that he was just trying to get a glimpse of his old love. But if he told the truth and Ellen found out, he'd have more trouble at home.

Just the thought of what Ellen might do gave him an idea. He couldn't tell her himself, but what if someone else told her that he'd been picked up stalking Addie because he still loved her? Maybe Ellen would be angry enough to leave. Steve, feeling like a doomed man, buried his face in his hands. No way was that going to happen, and it wouldn't work anyhow. Ellen was in this relationship for the long haul.

*****

Feeling the need for a nap, Addie was sitting at her desk wishing she hadn't eaten such a big lunch when the phone rang. Stifling a yawn, she answered, "Adeline Parker. May I help you?"

"Addie, I need your help."

Steve's voice chased away all thoughts of napping. Anger sent her out of her chair so abruptly that it tipped over. "Is this a joke, Steve? And if it is, it's not funny!"

Sweet Adeline

Just hearing Addie's voice took away his power of speech.

"Well?" Addie complained after hearing nothing but silence. "That's it? If you have nothing more to say, I'm hanging up. Goodbye, Steve!"

Still holding the phone, Addie backed up to a chair and collapsed. How dare he ask anything of her! He'd lost that right the day he introduced her to his new wife. That event was still too new and the wound was still too raw for her to have any desire to help him do anything.

After a few deep breaths to calm herself, curiosity took over. What kind of a mess had Steve gotten himself into that made him think she was the one who could help?

When her phone rang again, she was interested enough to answer it.

"This had better be good, Steve, or I'm hanging up again," was her greeting.

"No, no! Please, Addie. Don't hang up. They won't let me call back again."

She could hear voices in the background.

"What? Who won't let you? Where are you?"

"Uh, it seems…ah…you see," Addie knew Steve was running one hand through his hair, a common habit when he was nervous, "Oh, what the hell! I'm in jail."

"Jail?"

"Yes, jail. I'm allowed to make a call, and I chose to call you."

She snorted. "Am I supposed to be ecstatic that instead of calling your soul mate for help, you called me?"

Steve didn't answer. How could he explain why he'd been hanging around her neighborhood just trying to see her if he didn't confess that he'd made the biggest mistake of his life when he married Ellen? The police had picked him up after several neighbors had identified him as the guy they'd seen hanging around the area where a woman had been murdered.

"Addie, could you please get past hurt feelings long enough to get me out of here?"

"Hurt feelings? Is that all that's left of our two-year relationship? Just hurt feelings?"

"Please, Addie, hear me out. If you want to talk about it after this is all over, then so be it. Right now I need you to come down to the station and vouch for me."

So something bad had happened. "Steve, I need to know what you meant when you said 'when all this is over.' What kind of a mess have you gotten yourself into?"

"Please, Addie, I'd rather tell you when you get here. I was told to make this call a short one."

"Oh, no! You don't pull that one on me. You say you want me to vouch for you. Well, if you don't tell me what I have to vouch for, I'm not coming."

She heard Steve take a deep breath in resignation. "I guess I've forgotten how stubborn you can be. A murdered female jogger was found behind the big hedge a block down from where you live."

Addie gasped. "Murdered? My God! Do I know her?"

"Her name is Cindy. She was just jogging through your area, you wouldn't know her."

"But I've probably seen her! Oh, my God! A woman has been murdered and this is why you're in jail? Steve, what have you done?"

Now was the time.

"Addie, marrying Ellen was the biggest mistake I ever made." He stopped when he heard Addie gasp. "I miss you so much it's killing me! Sometimes it helps if I can just get a glimpse of you, and that's why I've been hanging around your area."

Addie's heart fluttered. *He still loves me, he still loves me!* kept running through her head until stark reality put a stop to it. Steve was married to someone else.

Hearing only silence on Addie's end, he tentatively asked, "Are you still there?"

She took a deep breath, and swallowed hard. "Yes, I'm still here. You're in jail because the police think you did it?"

"Several neighbors of yours reported seeing me in the crime area around the time of the murder."

"And how am I supposed to help you?"

"I need you to back up my story."

"What story?"

"That I'm a lovesick man with a broken heart."

She let out a short laugh. "And you really think that silly excuse will get you out of jail?"

Sweet Adeline

"Well, it's the truth, Addie!"

Addie chewed on her lower lip. Did she even want to help him? He sure hadn't hesitated to steamroll over her that day in front of the restaurant.

"Addie, please. I only have a few seconds left here."

Remembering that he'd been her best friend for two years, she gave in. "Okay. I'll do it. There are a few things I have to finish up here at the office, but I'll be there sometime in the next hour or so."

That really wasn't the truth. She didn't have any pressing matters to finish, but she liked the idea of making him stew in jail for another hour. Even though she knew she was acting petty, it felt good to make him suffer.

******

Finding a parking place at the jail was turning out to be a problem. It was while she was waiting for a slow-moving motorist to pull out of his parking spot that reality hit. She was going to see Steve. Really see him. Alone. Without Ellen.

Could she do this?

How could she erase the memories of shared holidays, the birthday celebrations or the weekends when they never ventured very far from the bedroom? History. She and Steve had two years of history. How can you walk away from that without looking back? Steve had. She thought she had, but now, knowing they were going to be face to face, her heart was racing. All Steve ever had to do was look into her eyes and she turned into mush. What if that happened today?

*****

Waiting for the fluttery sensation to start, Addie looked across the table at an orange-suited-handcuffed Steve. When nothing happened, she intentionally locked eyes with him.

Still, nothing.

Steve, on the other hand, was devouring her face with such longing in his eyes that she had to look away.

"Please tell me again how I'm going to get you out of here."

"Addie, they think I murdered her! I never laid eyes on that Cindy woman, and yet I'm being accused of killing her just because I've been hanging around your area and several of your neighbors recognized me."

"Really, Steve? You've been stalking me?"

47

"No, no! Not stalking, Addie. I just wanted to get a glimpse of you."

There was a look of disgust on her face when she said, "Do you know how sick that sounds? I should just go home and let you get yourself out of this mess."

"No, please stay! You see—," he stopped to gaze into her eyes. "You see, I miss you so damn much!" Reaching over, he grabbed her hand with his cuffed pair.

Addie pulled her hand away, stood up quickly, and stepped away from the table.

"Hear me out! Please!" he pleaded. "Marrying Ellen was the dumbest mistake of my entire life. Blame it on my ego, blame it on whatever you like, but she had done so much damage to me at the end of our senior year that seeing her again brought back all that agony. Only this time she wanted me, and that's all I could think about."

Addie sat back down. "But you did marry her, Steve. She's your wife and I'm entirely out of the picture."

"But you don't have to be out of the picture! Ellen is not how I remember her. How can I stay married to someone I don't even like?" He shuddered before he added, "Everything she does irritates me!"

Addie shook her head. "My mother used to say, 'You've made your bed, now lie in it.' You had a choice, and you chose Ellen. You shoved me out of your life without a second thought, so now be man enough to live with your decision, and don't you even dare think of me as a solution to your marital mess!"

"Addie, honey, I can't believe this is the real you talking. How can you forget what we had? Don't you want it back?"

She snorted. "Are you listening to yourself, Steve? You're the one who felt no qualms about ditching me! And no, I don't want us to be together." Surprised that she'd spoken the truth, she paused before she added, "You ruined it, and there's no fixing it."

Steve swallowed hard and took a deep breath. "I'm so sorry for what I've done, but more than that, I'm sad that you don't think we can ever reclaim what we had."

"My mother had another saying. Whenever I cried over a bad decision, she'd remind me of the old adage, 'You buttered your bread, now eat it.'" Taking a long breath to calm herself, she added, "Now what do I have to do to get you out of here?"

Sweet Adeline

"I'm not giving up, Addie. Somehow, I'm going to change your mind."

"No, you aren't."

He threw up his hands. "This isn't the end of us."

Addie's fist pounded the table. "Steve!"

"Okay, okay," Steve said waving off her anger and looking apologetic. "You just tell them that the reason I was hanging around the neighborhood was because I was hoping to see you."

Addie raised an eyebrow. "That's it?"

"It's true, Addie. I wanted to see you. I couldn't get through my day without seeing you. Since I knew that on days that we couldn't meet, you sometimes went home for lunch, I would go to your neighborhood during my lunch break, or I'd tell Ellen I had to work late and stop in your area on my way home after work."

"So what do you want from me? To say you were visiting me? I'm not lying for you Steve."

"No, I just want you to back up my love-sick story, because it's true."

Addie asked softly, "So you didn't kill anyone?"

There was a sad note in his voice when he answered. "I should be hurt that you'd even ask me that question, but no, I didn't."

She sighed in resignation. "I didn't think you did, but I had to ask. Steve, you are truly pathetic. But I'll do it."

*****

Back in his cell, Steve held his hands over his face to hide the tears that were running down his cheeks. What a mess he had made of his life. He'd lost Addie. He could feel the coldness that came over her when their eyes met. Her love for him was not there anymore. He was wiping his wet face on his sleeve when he heard a muffled sound from the next cell.

The man was weeping openly; tears and snot were running unchecked.

"Hey, man! You okay?" Steve asked.

"No, and I probably will never be okay again in this life."

"That bad?"

"Yeah. I've been accused of murdering my wife."

"Your wife? Did you do it?"

"Of course not! I love my—"

"Wait a minute," Steve interrupted. "Was your wife's name Cindy?"

The man nodded, his wet eyes narrow with suspicion. "Why would you ask me that?"

"Because I'm being accused of murdering her, too, and I've never met your wife. What's going on?"

Jeb relaxed. "I only wish I knew. The last time I saw her, she was leaving the house to go for an after-dinner jog. I went to sleep while waiting for her to return, and I didn't wake up until the police were at my door to tell me my wife had been murdered and to ask what kind of alibi I had for the last couple of hours. Can you believe that? They think I killed her, they think I killed my wife!"

"Is that all they have on you?" Steve asked.

"Well," Jeb admitted. "I had gone on a short walk before I took a nap."

"If that's all they have on you, they can only keep you in jail for forty-eight hours unless there are other compelling reasons to keep you."

"I thought my alibi was the only thing, but by the way one detective was talking, I think they've found something else. I didn't know there was something else to find."

*****

Whatever Addie had told the police, it had worked because it wasn't long before the guard came to release him.

As he left, Steve called out to the man he was leaving behind. "I'm sorry for your loss, and I'm sorry you're accused of killing her."

They walked out listening to a sobbing man crying over and over, "I didn't do it! I didn't do it! I didn't do it!"

The guard scoffed. "That's what they all say. It's almost always the husband!"

Chapter 17

Jeb tugged on the short cotton blanket that only covered half of his long body. Now that his feet and legs were warm, he tucked the thin-excuse-for-a-blanket over the rest of his body. He had just finished eating his first-ever jail dinner of lumpy mashed potatoes, gray meat and overcooked vegetables so he knew it was much too early to turn in for the night. But when you're locked-up there's nothing left to do.

To top it off, he was depressed. Most of his college friends were scattered all over the country and since he and Cindy hadn't been that friendly with the neighbors, there was no one he could call for support. Watching his jail mate walk out earlier today meant that not only was he all alone, now he was the lone suspect in his wife's murder. No one would tell him anything.

Now that he'd warmed up his shoulders, he pulled the blanket back down over his legs, doubled up the flat pillow, and stared at the ceiling. Life had become a nightmare. With no witnesses to back up his story, the walk and the time he claimed to be asleep on the couch wasn't working as an alibi. What else did the police have on him? They didn't know what the murder weapon was let alone find something that would indicate that he had anything to do with it. And to top it off, his do-nothing lawyer wasn't helping at all.

"Just don't say anything right now, Jeb," the scuzzball had told him. His lawyer didn't even believe him.

The sound of approaching footsteps made him curious enough to throw off the blanket and sit up. The guard and a scruffy-looking obviously inebriated man were heading for the empty cell next to his.

"Brought you some company," the guard said. "Jeb, meet George, the town drunk."

"Ah, come on now," George slurred. "Why did ya have to go and hurt my feelings?"

The guard closed and locked the door. "Have a good nap, George."

Jeb yelled at the back of the disappearing guard. "Hey, what did George do?"

"Nothing!" the guard yelled back. "He's just here to sleep it off. He gets into trouble when he's drunk."

Jeb turned to ask George how often he spent the night in jail, but the sound of loud snoring told him George was already asleep.

So much for company.

Jeb's struggle with the short blanket came to a halt when he had a thought so upsetting it knocked the air out of his lungs. It wouldn't be good if anyone found out that he was the writer of the published letter in the magazine. Admitting in that letter that he'd stalked his own wife was almost as good as a confession.

Jeb's groan woke George.

"Having trouble, Mate?" George inquired.

Jeb grunted in surprise.

"I wasn't really drunk. I just needed a place to sleep tonight because I got kicked out of the boarding house for hitting on the landlady."

Jeb actually laughed. "Do you end up in jail very often?"

"As often as I need to," George grinned.

"But what about tomorrow night? Will your landlady let you back in?"

"Yeah." George smirked. "She only kicked me out because another tenant saw me do it and she had to pretend she didn't like it."

There was silence for a bit. Finally Jeb asked, "Anything interesting going on out there?"

George scratched his head. "Nothing important. Oh yes, the big talk as I was being ushered past the office was about a jacket."

Jeb tried to keep his voice steady. "A jacket? What kind of jacket?"

"I think it has something to do with the murder of that housewife. What was her name? Cindy something. Yeah, that was her name."

Was the jacket the compelling evidence that was keeping him in jail past the forty-eight hours? Remembering that he hadn't been able to find his own because the dog had taken it, he asked, "Was it Cindy's jacket?"

Sweet Adeline

"No, from what I heard, it was the jacket of the guy who murdered her. I sure would hate to be in his shoes right now."

Chapter 18

The clanging of the cell door closing, the sliding noise of a turning key, and the sobs of a distraught Jeb Linden reverberated off the jail's cement walls. He was back in his cell after a brief and disturbing visit with his court-appointed legal counsel.

He was being charged with murder.

One neighbor had recognized the picture of him as the man he'd chased off his property with the water hose the day before, and near the murder scene they'd found the scattered remnants of a jacket that had a sewn-in tab with his name on it. The biggest blow was the two witnesses who swore they had seen him in the area at the time of the murder.

Jeb had kept his mouth shut. If he'd told them he had been following his wife in the attempt to find out if she was having an affair, that would be the same as confessing that he'd murdered her. But who would have wanted to hurt his wife? Could it have been the person she was having an affair with? Maybe they'd had an argument because Cindy wanted to end whatever it was. He'd like to think that was the reason for the argument that had gotten out of control and ended with Cindy dead.

The one thing he couldn't get out of his mind was the letter he'd mailed to that damn magazine. Yes, he thought his wife was cheating, and yes, he was stalking her. It would be the end of him if they somehow found out that he'd written the letter. It would give him motive.

Cindy. His beloved detail--oriented Cindy spent a lot of her time finding shortcuts for daily tasks. And gimmicks. She loved gimmicks. Drawers were full of junk she'd seen advertised on television and then had to have. Most of them didn't work, but that never stopped her from ordering anything that looked as if it would make life a bit easier or more interesting.

But it was the thing she'd done with envelopes that was causing his anxiety. To save time when paying bills, she'd taken a whole box of envelopes, stuck return labels in the left hand corner, and then put postage stamps in the other corner. In her mind, she'd just made the job of paying bills easier.

Sweet Adeline

Had he used one of those envelopes? That was the big question that was keeping him awake at night. If the magazine saw his name on the news, it would seem as if Jeb had listened to the advice and confronted his wife. Why hadn't he just asked Cindy about her jogging? Jeb covered his face with his hands, sobbing—how quickly life could turn on you.

Chapter 19

A familiar ping from her phone notified Addie that she had a text message. Since Steve was the only one who ever texted her, she hesitated to even check. If he still believed they had a future together, he had another think coming. Even if he divorced Ellen, there was not enough tea in China to bribe her back into a relationship with him. As far as she was concerned, he was dead meat. Dead, smelly dog meat.

The smile that lit up her face when she saw that the message was not from Steve turned to a frown when she noticed that it was from Mr. Lawson, a.k.a. Jim. Even though he was insisting that everyone in the office call him Jim, she was having trouble calling her boss by his first name. And along with being on a first-name basis, he was acting as if the Dr. Ask-Me-Anything secret the two of them shared gave him permission to hang around her office. Maybe she was seeing things, but she was pretty sure he'd winked at her yesterday. She loved her job, and she needed her job, but her boss's actions were beginning to look a little like sexual harassment.

After reading the text message, a request for yet another meeting to discuss the new column, she put her phone on the table and sighed. Following the first issue that had carried her reply to Worried in the Suburbs, the two of them had watched the mail, expecting to see dozens of letters from advice-seekers. There were replies, but not as many as they expected.

The unfinished computer game of Freecell beckoned for her attention. If she closed her computer, the loss of the game would wreck her unspoiled record of wins, and that was not going to happen.

It was only after the sound of bells and whistles that alerted the game-world that she'd won yet another one that she reluctantly knocked on her boss's door. He was blaming her for the reason the column had taken off like a lead balloon, insisting that it was her milk-toast reply that had killed the readers' interest. Maybe it was.

After all, she had been given instructions on how she was supposed to write the advice. The one thing he didn't want was a goody-goody advice column that sounded as if someone's kindly aunt had written it. He'd made it clear from the beginning that he wanted her reply to be offhand, sarcastic and caustic. That was not the way she'd written her reply to Worried, but he had seemed okay with it, at least enough to run it in the magazine.

Mr. Law...Jim...was slow to acknowledge her tap on his door. Maybe he wasn't eager to have another unpleasant meeting, either. At first, he'd laughed at her 'magic fingers' that had refused to type offensive words to Worried, but that was before the many days of waiting for requests that never appeared in the mail.

"Come in!"

Expecting to find a stern-faced boss waiting to give her bad news, she opened the door...and then quickly shut it.

"Is that you, Addie?"

"Yes."

Jim's voice was soft and seductive. "Please come in."

"Uh, Mr. Laws...Jim?"

"Yes?"

In a cautious voice she asked, "What's going on in there?"

He chuckled. "Why don't you come in and find out?"

What she'd seen when she first peeked in was a dark office except for a dim flickering light. Wait a minute. First there was the secret, then there was the wink, and now his office was looking like some kind of a seductive trap. Was her boss hitting on her?

She pushed on the door and entered.

The first thing she saw was that a burning candle was the dim flickering light, the second thing she saw was that the candle was on a cake, and the third thing she saw was her boss's face that could be leering, although it was hard to tell in the dark room.

"I'd sing to you, Addie, but I can't carry a tune."

Shocked beyond words, her mouth was moving but nothing was coming out.

"Don't tell me you forgot," he chuckled.

She frowned. "Forgot what?"

"Your birthday!"

"Oh, for heaven's sake!" she collapsed. "My birthday!"

"How can you forget your own birthday?"

"I...I...guess," she thought for a moment. "I guess it's because I don't have anyone to remind me."

"No one?" he asked, suddenly interested.

She shook her head. "No one."

"No family?"

"Just a sister in Ohio."

"Uh…that is…I don't mean to pry, but what happened to the steady boyfriend?"

"He's history."

History? His heart skipped a beat. "Permanent history or is it just temporary history until you kiss and make up?"

She shrugged. "He married someone else. Is that permanent enough?"

The seed of hope that had taken root in his heart the first time he'd laid eyes on her quivered. With competition out of the way, maybe there was a chance for him after all.

Turning his head so that she couldn't see the pleased expression on his face, he managed to sound sympathetic. "I'm so sorry to hear that, Addie! Are you okay?"

Acting as if it weren't a big deal, she just nodded, shrugged, cleared her throat and asked, "Jim, what's really going on?"

This cynical reaction was not what he'd hoped for. His plot to have her finally accept him as something other than her boss had flopped. How was he going to get out of this without looking like an idiot?

Thinking fast, he spit out the first thing his spinning brain came up with. "It's a birthday surprise! The cake is the start of an office birthday tradition."

"And the candle?"

"Oh, I don't know. It just seems right to have a candle on a birthday cake."

She blew out a held breath. "Whew! For a while I was kinda creeped out."

Hoping that his face wasn't red, he reached around her, found the wall switch, turned on the light, blew out the candle, and said, "Now, about the next issue—"

Chapter 20

As soon as the door closed on the departing birthday girl, Jim, a.k.a. James Allen Lawson III, buried his face in his hands. Well now, wasn't that special. His little plan had backfired big time. In her own words, it had "creeped her out." Had it upset her to the point of filing harassment charges against him? Just the thought of that happening was making him sweat.

His little failed experiment had dug another hole. Now he had to put the cake with Addie's name on it by the coffee station knowing that from now on he'd have to supply a cake every time someone in the office had a birthday. Being the boss of his dad's business was becoming a pain in the ass.

In a way, Jim had inherited the magazine from his father. But it was the original James Allen Lawson who, by hard work and sacrifice, had produced the wealth that had enabled his only son to become an unproductive playboy. James the Second and his fourth wife had been living on his yacht, a gift from his dad, somewhere on the Mediterranean when the old man died, leaving him everything. The assets he welcomed, but not the failing magazine business.

James the Second thought magazines were going the way of the dodo bird, and what better way to hasten its demise than to hang it around the neck of James Allen Lawson III, the only offspring of his many marriages? True, he'd never met James the Third. Beth, his first wife, hadn't known she was pregnant when she bailed out of their short marriage. What a fuss she'd made over finding him in bed with the live-in maid. He claimed the maid had just crawled into bed with him, but when Beth refused to believe him, he had accused her of not having a sense of humor. She did not respond well to that. He was a rich man's son, used to getting his own way, so he wasn't really upset when she'd left. He thought she'd be back in a few days, and already he was eagerly anticipating the hot make-up sex that was sure to happen when she returned. But Beth never came back.

When James the Second offered his son the magazine, he hoped he had a better sense of humor than his mother. How qualified he was for the job didn't matter. He did know that the boy had a college degree because he'd paid for it. Whatever happened afterwards wasn't much of a concern to James the Second, as long as he could remain floating in the sun on the Mediterranean.

*****

Jim didn't know much of his family history. His father was just a mythical person whose monthly checks allowed him and his mother to scrape by as long as she held down two jobs.

Armed with his new diploma, Jim's excitement at being thrown into the real world was short lived. He, along with many of his university friends, found that jobs weren't out there waiting for them when they graduated.

Jim felt awful about being unemployed. Watching his mother working so hard was upsetting. He'd been job searching for several months when the letter from his father arrived. This was a first. Outside of financing his university degree, never before had his dad ever acknowledged his existence. Not a birthday card, not a phone call, nothing. But something had changed, because in his shaking hand, he was holding a letter from him.

Jim sat and stared at something he'd never seen before: his dad's handwriting. The envelope felt hot in his hands. His own father had addressed it, and even licked the glue to seal it. After all the years of silence, what had he put inside it? Jim's heart was thumping inside his chest as he tore the envelope open.

Minutes later after reading the letter, he was really in shock. The father that he'd never seen was offering him the management position of one of his businesses…a magazine that he'd seen his mother reading. His dad was offering him a job!

At last he had a chance to be noticed. If he worked hard and made the business profitable, maybe his father would pay attention to him. Oh, he'd read all about him on the Internet, and there had been pictures, but he was always in a group shot which made it hard to make out his facial features. According to the Internet, a widow's peak is a dominant inherited trait; no one in his mother's family had one, so his must have come from his father. That had made him wonder if his dad had dark brown eyes, too. Sometimes he'd catch his mother looking at him with a sad look on her face. If he really did look like his dad, was she remembering the man who had done something so terrible that she'd left him? Who was his mother seeing when she looked at him?

Sweet Adeline

Before he replied to the offer, he checked out *Your World* online; he liked what he found. While he was at it, he searched and read articles about how to be a good manager. Like a thirsty sponge, he soaked up all the information, especially the part about not getting chummy with those he was managing.

But that was before he met Addie.

Chapter 21

There she is, the bitch!

Bile rose in Ellen's throat as she watched Addie rush into the jail. It was true, then. Steve was in trouble but he hadn't called her. Swallowing hard, she threw her silent cell phone into her backpack.

Overcoming her fear of riding her bicycle on the heavily traveled peninsula road into town hadn't been easy, but once she saw the police driving off with Steve in the back seat of the squad car, she didn't have a choice.

Her days of following Steve on her bike had been filled with fear that he would catch her spying, but she had to see his betrayal with her own eyes. Watching her lovesick husband stalking Addie was painful, but the emptiness in his eyes when he looked at her, his wife, hurt worse. The paradise she and Steve had found was no more. Addie had ruined it.

Now, he was in trouble, and instead of calling her, he'd called Addie.

*****

She'd almost stayed home the day of the reunion. Why should she put herself into a situation where old classmates would be asking questions that she didn't want to answer? Her life since graduation wasn't something she'd ever think of sharing.

But she did go, and once there, she found a secluded corner seat where she could observe her former classmates talking to each other, most likely painting verbal rosy pictures of their postgraduate lives. She had no doubt that some of their stories were made up.

And then Steve stepped into the room.

Her heart skipped a beat. Would he notice her in the corner? Holding her breath, she had waited. Their last date had ended badly when, without a word, she'd slipped out of his arms in the middle of a slow dance and disappeared for an hour. Parting words had been harsh that prom night so long ago. That was not the way she'd envisioned the ending of their semester fling, but because of her family's activities, she knew there had to be an ending. Realizing that had made every minute spent with him bittersweet.

Sweet Adeline

Because of him, the last part of her senior year had been the happiest time of her life. Never in a million years had she ever dreamed that the big man on campus would look at her, let alone become her steady boyfriend. But he had, and she'd loved every minute of it. It was disappointing that the early breakup meant that they wouldn't be spending the summer together before Steve headed off for college. But things have a way of working out. What had happened to her in the hour that she'd disappeared would have finished them anyway.

Ellen was so deep in thought that she almost missed Addie leaving the jail. Whatever she'd been in there for, it hadn't taken long. At least Steve hadn't left with her. That meant he was still in there. Good. The cheating son-of-a-bitch could rot for all she cared.

An alarm in her head sounded when the familiar feeling of monthly cramps gripped her, announcing the beginning of her period. How could that be? True, Steve hadn't touched her after she made the announcement that she'd quit taking the pill, but there had been a lot of sexual activity before she made the stupid statement. Being pregnant was her final game card. Steve, being the honorable man that he was, would never desert her if she were carrying his child. Now what?

If it weren't for Addie, she and Steve could make this work. After all, the fact that they were married had to count for something.

Ellen straddled her bicycle and headed for home. Addie was probably going back to work, so there was no chance for her to see the bike rider peddling north on the peninsula road.

The ride home gave her a lot of time to think about ways the bitch could be removed from the picture.

Chapter 22

Lucky for her, Addie saw her boss heading toward her in time to hastily shut the top on her computer. No sense in advertising the fact that she was filling the time by searching the Internet for interesting things to read.

The Dr. Ask-Me-Anything feature hadn't taken off, thanks to the too-sweet answer she had written for Worried. Even though the letter had probably cost her the job, she couldn't help wondering if he had taken her advice. The envelope with his return address was still in her bottom desk drawer. Did she have follow-up rights as Dr. Ask-Me-Anything?

As Mr. Lawson got closer, she could see that there was a smile on his face. For days he'd been walking around looking like his dog had died. Whatever had been bothering him was gone.

"Look what came in the mail today!" he chortled while throwing six envelopes onto her desk.

Her eyes widened. "All for Dr. Ask-Me-Anything?"

"Every one of them!"

The relief in his voice was obvious. He was the only one who knew that his dad was threatening to close down the failing business. "Who reads magazines when they have the Internet?" he'd asked during their phone conversation three weeks ago. After much pleading, his dad had agreed to give him a few more issues to prove himself. Jim was betting it all on the new Dr. Ask-Me-Anything section.

"Have you read them?" she asked.

"Yes, and there are some good ones in there. I think most of them were written by fraternity guys, but I don't really care who writes the letters. Just remember I'm looking for the zing, the barb and the ridiculous. Make me proud!"

She opened the first envelope.

*****

James Allen Lawson the Third tried to concentrate on the lengthy email from James Allen Lawson, the Second. It was not the kind of message one would imagine a dad would write to his son. There was nothing personal in it, there was no warmth, and no

Sweet Adeline

inkling of a family tie; there were just cold facts and numbers. The magazine was failing and it was obvious that James the Second really didn't care. To his credit, he was quick to point out that he was placing no blame on James the Third for the failure; the market for most magazines had dried up.

Jim saw his one chance to please his dad evaporating. Under his supervision, articles had been better written, the subjects *had* been more interesting, and the pictures *had* been more arresting. It hadn't helped. Today's financial section of the paper reported the failure of two more periodicals. According to his dad, it was just a matter of time, so why not just quietly close down the business? Jim's fight for the life of the magazine had gotten him a short reprieve.

He lowered the email printout and allowed his eyes to seek Addie's bent head. Funny the way things had worked out. At the beginning, the Dr. Ask-Me-Anything idea had been just a ruse to get to work with her. Based on the small amount of feedback he'd received from just the one response, he was disappointed, but he still believed that her advice column might just be the difference between success and failure. Whatever the outcome, Jim knew that he'd fallen hard. It didn't help that Addie saw him as her boss, and nothing more. Watching her trying to call him by his first name would be funny if it weren't so painful.

Chapter 23

Ellen absentmindedly played with the ray of sun that reflected off the rings on her left hand. The chain of events that had placed those rings on her finger was unexpected and unplanned.

Sure, she'd missed Steve after their prom night parting, but her heart hadn't been broken; she had other irons in the fire. It was fortunate for her that right after graduation her family fled the state.

The one-hour disappearance the night of the prom had caused more than just the break-up; she'd gotten pregnant. It was her dad who had set up the meeting. He needed her, he'd told her, to "sweet-talk" a guy who was threatening to ruin him. Apologizing for interrupting her prom night, he pleaded for her to do this one thing for him. She was his last hope, he explained. If the guy snitched, then the whole family had to disappear.

"Sweet-talk" the guy was all her dad told her to do, but what happened was so much more than that. Is that what her dad had offered him? Sex with his daughter in exchange for keeping his mouth shut?

The guy snitched anyway.

If she and Steve had been messing around, she would have had no qualm about naming him the father. Unfortunately, Good Guy Steve had insisted on being the guardian of her virginity. What a laugh that was.

It had been her first abortion.

*****

For the past hour Ellen had been sitting in the privacy of Steve's car gathering the courage to make a call on her cell phone to Albert Linder, her old partner in nefarious scams. Before they hooked up, he'd worked for her father. Their last venture had backfired, and because Albert had covered for her, he'd been sent to jail.

She couldn't count the times she'd chickened out with just one more number to be touched to complete the call. No one likes to hear "I told you so."

"You'll be back," Albert had said the last time she'd visited him in jail. "I know you better than you know yourself, Ellen."

Sweet Adeline

"This time it's different! This is my chance to make something of my life!"

He snorted. "You can't make a silk purse out of a sow's ear."

"If I'm a sow's ear, what does that make you?"

"Your husband. Or have you forgotten?"

"I'm trying to."

"So, you are just going to pretend that I don't exist? There's a word for a woman who marries more than one man, you know."

"You gonna squeal on me?"

He studied her face before he answered. "Depends."

"Depends? What kind of an answer is that?"

"Depends on what's in it for me."

"What's that supposed to mean?"

"Guess you'll have to wait to find out."

She glared at him. He grinned at her.

"Are we really married?" she asked quietly.

He shrugged. "Hell if I know."

"I know we had a ceremony, but just because the kid said he was a preacher, doesn't mean he was."

He laughed. "That was a wild scene! The drunk in the holding cell was a pretty good singer. 'Oh Promise Me' sounded real professional until he got to the high note."

"I've been doing some research," Ellen said. "It seems that the ceremony is just for show. The one with the authority to perform marriages has to register it or it's not a marriage."

*****

Ellen picked up the cell and touched the last number. She closed her eyes and pictured the ringing phone in her dead parents' old house where Albert had been living since his release from jail. They weren't married, she'd told him. She'd described in detail her unsuccessful search for their marriage record. However, for old time's sake and the goodness of her heart, she would allow him to live in the old house.

Was he curious enough to check for himself? Her whole future hung on that question. The kid *had* been a preacher, the drunk in the holding cell *had* witnessed it, and the marriage *had* been registered.

What was the chance that anyone would uncover the fact that she really was married to Albert?

He picked up on the second ring.

"I didn't expect a call this soon," he gloated.

"Don't be an asshole, Albert."

"Whoa! The name's Earl, remember?"

"Ha. Albert Richard Linder, you can change your name all you want, but you're still an asshole."

"Well, I guess if you're still a sow's ear, I can be an asshole."

She paused before she asked cautiously, "What makes you think I've messed up?"

"Are you going to tell me that you called me just to say hello? I don't think so."

She closed her eyes. He knew her so well.

"Al…Earl?"

"Here it comes."

"I need your help."

Damn him! He was laughing.

"I told you so!" He laughed harder.

"Stop it!" she hissed. "I hate it when you gloat!"

"Ah, Ellen, you are *so* predictable! What do you need?"

"I need you to get rid of two things."

"Big things, little things, stolen things, bodies? Please, no bodies."

Silence.

He sighed. "So there are bodies."

"Not yet, but maybe."

"You said two things. What's the other one?"

"I need you to get rid of a jacket."

"A jacket?" There was disgust in his voice. "Are you shoplifting again? I thought we'd gotten past that phase of your life."

"I didn't shoplift it. I was riding my bike…." She paused and swallowed hard. "Honest, I only meant to knock the jogger out so that I could steal her really cool jacket. But I hit her too hard, and she's dead. I need to get rid of it."

"For God's sake Ellen! You killed someone? You stripped a jacket off a dead body?"

"Calm down! I told you it was an accident! Anyhow, no one saw me do it."

Sweet Adeline

"Ellen, you and I haven't been angels, but we never hurt anyone; we just emptied their bank account. You've gotten yourself into a real mess this time!"

"No sermons, please."

"I'll quit preaching sermons when you start acting like an adult! Sure, I covered for you back when you were doing all those crazy things, but I thought you'd grown up. To be honest, I still live in fear that some of those capers are going to come back and bite us one day."

"Earl, just knock it off! I'm trying, I really am, but what's done is done! Are you going to help me or not?"

"Sorry. Let me get this straight. You don't need me to get rid of the body?"

"No, her husband is being held for her murder."

"Ellen, Ellen," he scolded.

"Earl, Earl," she mimicked.

"Okay, I can handle getting rid of the jacket. What's the other thing you want me to get rid of?"

"Her name is Addie."

Chapter 24

Addie scanned the last advice reply she'd just written for the next issue. What surprised her wasn't the fact that it was well written because she was an excellent writer, but it puzzled her as to where all the sarcasm, belittling and offensive sentences were coming from. The readers were eating it up, sales were soaring, and Mr. Law…Jim was walking around with a big grin on his face. It bothered her that he was constantly hanging around her office while she was trying to work. Not only did it inhibit her creative ability, it gave fuel to the office rumors that something was going on between the two of them. And there was most certainly nothing going on from her perspective.

It was past closing time and the office was empty. Needing peace and quiet to finish the replies, she'd stayed at her computer after everyone had gone, including her boss. When she was satisfied about what she'd written and rewritten, she was ready to leave for the day. Grabbing her coat and purse, she was heading for the door when it burst open and a man, obviously in a hurry, rushed passed her.

"Sir," she called, "the office is closed. Are you here to see someone?"

When the man turned around to face her, Addie found herself looking into eyes as blue as the sky on a cloudless summer day. And dimples. In both cheeks.

"Oh?" the man exclaimed. "But I had an appointment!"

She was having trouble breathing. "With whom?"

His searching eyes scanned the office, and then with the look of a humbled and confused man, he asked, "Uh, this is the law office of Walls, Dallas and Murphy isn't it?"

"Sir, you got off the elevator too soon. The law office is on the seventh floor. This is the sixth."

He dropped his head and looked at the floor. "How stupid of me!"

"No, no!" she laughed. "Not stupid at all."

"Thank you," he said, holding out his hand. "By the way, I'm Earl Dixon."

Sweet Adeline

She hesitated just a split second before she accepted his hand. "I'm Adeline Parker."

He smiled at the attractive green-eyed redhead who was holding his hand.

This was going to be fun.

*****

Jim swung into the gym's parking lot, pleased to see there were plenty of parking spots. That meant the machines would not be in heavy use. He hated waiting around for his turn, which happened more times than he liked. The only gym he could afford was this small one. Maybe, just maybe, if his publication continued to stay afloat, his dad would give him a raise. The first thing he'd do would be to apply for a membership at the new spa in town. He grimaced at the thought because there was no way a small raise would get him into something as fancy as that. But since dreams were free, why not dream about trading in his old green junker with the smashed left fender for something better? Dream on!

It was hard work and it certainly wasn't dreaming that had gotten him into his present physical shape. Someday he'd have enough money to afford clothes that would show the result of his hard work, and then maybe Addie would look at him differently. But she was a dream that money couldn't buy. Hell, she still was uncomfortable calling him anything other than Mr. Lawson.

Life was looking so much better since the Dr. Ask-Me-Anything feature had taken off. Like Addie, he was pretty sure that most of the letters they were receiving were written by frat boys, but he really didn't care.

Today's financial report noted that two more magazines had called it quits; he gloried in the fact that his wasn't one of them.

Chapter 25

When you're as good-looking as Earl, following someone without being detected is almost impossible. Trying to figure out Addie's schedule so that bumping into her "accidentally" wouldn't seem planned was causing him a bit more trouble than he was used to. And on top of that, he was becoming more curious about the tall blond guy who kept showing up. Was he following Addie, too? Wait a minute. Didn't Ellen say that Steve was tall and blond? So, she hadn't exaggerated; her husband was still in love with Addie. No wonder Ellen wanted the woman removed from the picture.

He could understand Steve's inability to let go. Hell, he still felt connected to Ellen who he'd met while he was involved in one of her dad's ongoing scams. They never had any romantic feelings for each other, just mutual appreciation. When one of their joint activities would get them into trouble with the law, he made sure that Ellen's name never came up. She didn't even have a police record because he refused to rat on her.

Finding him despondent and depressed on one of her prison visits, she was trying to console him when a visiting preacher, misreading her sympathy as love, offered to marry them.

No way was the young kid's claim to be a minister valid, so they played along. Music was supplied by the drunken guy in the holding cell, the kid said the magic words, they signed some kind of form, and voila, Earl was no longer depressed. It made a good story to share with friends. He had to admit that he felt relieved when Ellen recently told him that she'd checked and there was no record of their marriage.

Ah, there Addie was, coming out of the store empty handed. And there he was, the tall blond guy who was trying to stay out of sight behind a parked car. Interesting.

Time to get the show on the road.

*****

There it was again, that tingly feeling that caused the hair on her arms to stand up. Her mother used to say it meant that someone was walking on your grave when that happened.

Sweet Adeline

Her musings were cut short by the sound of things hitting the sidewalk. Turning around, she saw a man who was stooping down to retrieve items that had fallen out of a ripped grocery bag. Potatoes, apples and a head of lettuce were heading for the gutter.

"Here, let me help you!" she exclaimed.

The man grunted. "Good thing I didn't buy eggs today!"

"You're going to need a new bag. I'll run into the store and get one for you."

"I'd really appreciate…hey, wait a minute!" the man's face lit up. "I've seen you before!"

Addie's eyes widened. The sky-blue eyes, the dimpled cheeks, "Earl?"

He nodded, dropped his eyes, and while trying to look apologetic, muttered, "You got me. I remember your face, but not your name."

"Adeline, it's Adeline."

"Of course!" he grinned. "How could I have forgotten?"

"No big deal. I'll be right back with a bag that has a bottom," she laughed as she disappeared into the store.

That left Earl with time to revel in the success of his contrived accidental meeting. When you're good, it's easy.

Addie had to wait her turn in the check-out line to ask for a bag. That gave her time to think about the extremely handsome Earl. The fiasco with Steve had left her with a bitter taste in her mouth, making her wonder if all men were like that. Up until now, she'd had no interest in finding out. But Earl? He was hard to ignore, and running into him twice seemed like a sign.

When all the items were picked up and in the new bag, Addie accepted Earl's lunch invitation.

Steve watched the woman he loved walk off with a guy he'd never seen before.

Chapter 26

The only booth available was in the back corner of the restaurant. As Addie and Earl followed the hostess, eyes were drawn to the extremely handsome couple. Were they celebrities? The slim red- headed woman was too short to be a model but she could be an actress, and the man? The mouths of the women were watering, and it wasn't for the food. The man was lethally handsome. The high cheekbones, regal nose and seductive mouth were just the beginning. His shirt was pulled taunt over the muscles on his body and gave the impression that it was going to burst at the seams at any moment. At least every female onlooker secretly hoped so.

Unaware of the eyes that were following them, the couple sat down, accepted the menu from the hostess and pretended to read it.

Addie was having trouble breathing. She had never before seen a man as appealing as Earl. Unable to keep her eyes on the menu, she looked across the table and found him staring at her. Their eyes met and she melted into the cushion of the booth.

Earl smiled at her; sometimes things were too easy.

*****

Steve peered into the restaurant's window, his eyes searching for Addie's red hair. Finding them in the back corner, he tortured himself for several minutes watching Addie's animated face. He had to look away when he saw her hand reach out and touch the guy flirtatiously. After he gained his composure and looked back, they were holding hands.

If only he could go back to that high school reunion and rewrite history! He closed his eyes and relived the scene that had brought him to where he was today.

*****

Who goes to these stupid reunions anyway? Steve asked himself. Certainly not his three singing mates. They were the reason he was spending a weekend away from Addie and they hadn't bothered to show up. Jackson had started the "Let's all go to the reunion" plea back when he was trying to hook up with the class's beauty queen who was between husbands. Dean and Ray were the

Sweet Adeline

ones who had talked Steve into going, but when Jackson called it off because the beauty queen had gone back to her first husband, they hadn't bothered to tell him. Steve was working on a few choice comments to heap upon their heads the next time he saw them.

Since there was no reason to stay, he might as well skip the evening's scheduled activities and head home. How surprised Addie would be tonight when he sang to her outside her bedroom window. Knowing that would mean he would be spending the night with her made him eager to start the trip home. His decision made, he took one last look over the crowd.

His eyes landed on a familiar face.

His world tilted.

It had never entered his mind that she might show up at the reunion.

Her disappearance had been quick and untraceable, almost as if she'd been a dream. But here she was, the girl he'd obsessed about all through his college years. His eyes drank in the woman who in the blink of an eye had escaped from his life, leaving him with a shattered heart. Her long hair was gone, she'd gained quite a few pounds, and she was taller than he'd remembered, but the essence of her hadn't changed. It was his Ellen.

Chattering voices faded into nothing as the two of them faced each other. The years fell away as Steve gazed into Ellen's eyes. Even though he hadn't seen her since that night, his heart remembered. After all, she was the one who'd broken it.

When he pulled Ellen into his arms and kissed her, it was as if Addie had never existed.

*****

Despondent, Steve turned away from the window and headed home. Ellen was probably there cooking one of her awful dinners. To be honest, they probably weren't that bad, but when everything she did irritated him, that's the way they seemed to him.

How had he ever thought he had feelings for this woman? She was crude, her personal hygiene was iffy, and her manner of speaking was coarse. These were things he hadn't recognized when they dated back in high school. Maybe because she was different then. He remembered silky hair, soft perfumed skin and sweet breath that always smelled of peppermint.

The closer he got to home, the feeling that the walls of his world were closing in on him grew stronger. Ellen would be waiting, expecting a hug and a kiss from her new husband. Even thinking about it made him break out in a sweat. He couldn't stand touching her, and the fact that he didn't know when she had stopped taking the pill made him light-headed. Remembering all the wild sex the two of them had engaged in at the beginning, it was possible that she could already be pregnant. If she were, he'd be trapped for life. She still didn't know about his little stint in the local jail. Again he wondered if she ever found out, would it upset her enough to leave?

He chalked that thought up to just wishful thinking.

Chapter 27

Addie couldn't keep her eyes off her lunch companion. Where had this Adonis been hiding all her life? Her sandwich remained untouched on her plate; how could she eat when all she wanted to do was to think of those full luscious lips on her own? Earl continued to entertain her with funny stories until he noticed she wasn't eating.

"Something wrong?" he asked her.

Addie blushed crimson, hoping her face hadn't revealed what she was thinking. "No," she laughed nervously.

Pointing to her untouched sandwich, he asked, "Would you like to order something else?"

She looked down at her plate, surprised that her bacon, lettuce and tomato sandwich had no bites taken out of it. "N...n...no, the sandwich is fine. I guess I was just so interested in your stories I forgot to eat."

"That interesting, eh?" he grinned. "And I haven't even told you the best ones."

Leaning across the table, she was surprised how husky her voice sounded when she asked, "Will you promise to tell them to me?"

Earl put down his sandwich, flashed his dimpled smile at her and moved toward her. Their faces were almost touching when he whispered, "I have a picture in my head of us snuggling together by the fireplace while I tell them to you."

Edgy silence. Her flirtation suddenly fled, her body tensed, and her fingers clenched the edge of the table. She shifted her weight side to side, a nervous smile on her face. Had she heard right? This hunk wanted to snuggle with *her*? "Earl?"

His eyebrows danced, "Yes?"

Addie took a deep breath, gathering courage. "Did you just ask to see me again?"

The devil was in his smile when he replied, "I don't know. Did I?"

"Sounded like it."

"Well, what if I did?"

Feeling like a child who had just been offered a treat, she blurted, "Well, if you *did* ask to see me again, I would have to say yes. *If* you were asking."

"Great!" He clapped his hands. "Are you free tonight?" Leaning back in his chair, he took a good look at Addie. This was the woman Steve had thrown away for Ellen? Idiot!

Seeing the intensity of his eyes, she didn't trust her voice to answer; she just nodded. What she really wanted to do was stand on top of the table and announce that she, Adeline Parker, had a date with the yummiest hunk in the whole world. Of course, a sane person wouldn't do anything like that, but right now she was feeling anything but sane.

Earl was a pro when it came to seducing women, so he wasn't surprised at Addie's response. What surprised him was *his* reaction to her. Ellen would not be happy with this development. But then Ellen wasn't planning right if she thought Steve would be hers if Addie wasn't around. He'd seen the love-stricken face of the tall blond man who was following Addie; he still loved her. Removing her from the picture wouldn't make him love Ellen. In fact, if she went missing, a devastated Steve wouldn't give Ellen a second thought. So why remove Addie?

He wouldn't.

His decision made, he smiled. He was tired of cleaning up Ellen's messes. The jacket would be easy to get rid of, but Addie was going to be his for as long as he wanted to play with her. That's when he noticed the concerned look on Addie's face. "Something wrong?"

"Maybe. Are we taking this thing a little too fast? Cuddling by the fireplace? Really? Tonight will just be our first date."

He gave her a dimpled smile, waved his hand dismissively, and said, "Hey, we're both adults! We can go as slow or as fast as we want, plus it's technically our second date."

Addie shrugged. "I suppose you're right." She looked at the time on her cell phone. "I only have a few more minutes before I have to get back to work."

"Yeah, at that magazine place where I got off the elevator on the wrong floor. What do you do there?"

"I'm a writer."

Earl leaned back in his chair. "Wait a minute. I've never known a writer! What kind of writer?"

Sweet Adeline

"Right now I write mostly drivel."

"Really? Drivel?"

"Light, fluffy articles about school lunches, table settings, party planning. Things like that." Addie scrunched up her nose in disgust.

"Uh, so you don't like writing drivel." Earl guessed.

She laughed. "Like most writers, I think I'm talented enough to write a best seller...my professors thought so, too. But I need to pay my bills, so I write space-filler for *Your World.*"

"*Your World?* I've read that magazine a few times."

"Recently?"

"Yeah, the latest issue, in fact. There's a new advice column that caught my eye."

"Did you like it?" Addie struggled to keep her face straight.

He laughed. "Whoever Dr. Ask-Me-Anything really is, I'd like to meet him. He's refreshingly irreverent, disrespectful, rude and flippant. Do you know him?"

She shook her head. "No one knows who he is. It's a big secret."

With a devilish grin on his face, he teased, "It's you, isn't it? I'd bet money on it."

Sticking out her tongue, she wiggled it at him. "Then you'd lose."

He threw back his head and laughed. "Addie, you are the most refreshing thing I've run into in a long time. Tell you what. Tonight I'll even throw in a home-cooked dinner before story time."

"You're going to cook?"

Since he intended to buy take-out at the best restaurant in town and then transfer the food to his own pans, he grinned, "You are going to be *so* impressed!"

She extended her hand across the table. "Sounds like a good plan. Meet me by the elevator bank in my building at 6:00?"

"I'll be there!"

An unfamiliar emotion swept over him as he watched her walk away. He didn't put a name on it. He just enjoyed it.

Ellen was not going to like this.

*****

The spring in her step and the smile on her face lasted until she stepped off the elevator on the sixth floor and found a frowning boss waiting for her.

"You're late, Addie," he announced in a loud voice, drawing the attention of the other workers who were already seated at their desks.

The second hand was just making it to the number six when she glanced at the clock; he was making a fuss over half a minute. Unfortunately, he'd eaten his lunch in the same restaurant as Addie and Earl. Watching the two of them laughing and enjoying each other was a hard thing to swallow along with his lunch.

Trying to look repentant, she hung her head. "I'm sorry *Mr. Lawson*. It won't happen again."

Damn. He'd just wrecked all the progress he'd made over a tardy thirty seconds, but it's hard to be reasonable when your heart is bleeding.

Lunch had been hell.

Chapter 28

The smell was getting to him. Even with all the windows closed, Earl could feel the smell of rot filling his car. Feeling uncomfortable, he drummed his fingers on the steering wheel wondering why in the world Ellen had instructed him to meet her at the dump.

Her directions had been very precise, so where was she, and why was she a half hour late? Checking the map she had drawn for him, Earl reassured himself that he'd correctly made all the right twists and turns. Without her detailed drawing, finding the dirt road behind the town's dump would have been impossible. But why here?

Five more minutes. After that, he was getting out of this God-forsaken place and Ellen would just have to find someone else to clean up her mess.

Four minutes later, he'd put the car into gear preparing to leave when the sound of squealing brakes announced her arrival. He watched as a disheveled and frantic Ellen jumped out of her car and headed for his.

Earl was pissed. He was here only because he had agreed to do her a favor, and no way was he going to let her get away without saying something. Ready to unload his displeasure on her for being late, he reached over and opened the side door. Before he had a chance to say a word, Ellen threw herself into the car and burst into tears.

"Whoa!" he exclaimed. "What's with the tears?"

"I'm not p…p…pregnant!" she sobbed.

Earl looked puzzled. "Not pregnant? And that's a problem?"

Ellen hiccupped. "Yes, it's a big problem!"

"I don't know whether to laugh or cry along with you. Why is it important for you to be pregnant?"

"Because," she paused to blow her nose, "I think that's the only way I'm going to make Steve stay with me. He doesn't know that I'm aware that he spent some time in jail for stalking Addie. I thought that would scare him, but he's back at it." New tears rolled down her cheeks. "H…h…he still loves her," she wailed.

And I can see why, Earl thought. Aloud he said, "You've only been married a short time, Ellen. How do you know that you won't get pregnant in the near future?"

"Ha! That's a laugh! Steve hasn't touched me since I told him that I'd quit taking the pill." She hung her head. "Actually, I quit taking them right after we were married. I also told him that I was pretty sure that I was already pregnant."

"Why would you tell him that?"

"Because I thought I was! There at the beginning, sex was nonstop." She quit talking when Earl put his hands over his ears.

"Too much!" he yelled. "I don't need to hear about your sex life!"

She looked at him, surprised. "Earl, when did you start being prudish about sex? You never used to be."

"Drop the subject, Ellen."

"No, I won't! Remember I asked you to do a couple of things for me? Well, I just came up with two more requests."

"Uh, about the original requests. We need to have a discussion about one of them."

"You aren't taking back your offer, are you?" she sounded anxious. "The jacket should be easily gotten rid of. We're right here by the dump and I have it with me."

"Before we go any further, what are the new requests?"

He hadn't noticed before, but Ellen had brought a large bag with her. Now he watched as she opened it so that he could see a jacket, along with what looked like a baseball bat with suspicious dark rusty stains on it.

His eyes bulged. "Don't tell me that's what you used to hit the jogger over the head?"

She nodded.

"And you haven't gotten rid of it before this?"

"Does it look like I have?"

"Okay, so that was a dumb question, but a bat? Where the hell did you get a bat? You were riding a bike!"

She sniffed. "Oh, you know silly old me! I always carry a bat around in case I want to bash someone's head in."

"Ellen, be serious. Where did you get it?"

"It was just there on the grass where some kid must have dropped it. I'd already spotted the jacket so I just picked it up."

Sweet Adeline

"Ellen, Ellen," he shook his head in disgust. "Why are you carrying it around?"

"To give to you, stupid! You can get rid of this when you get rid of the jacket."

He shook his head. "No way! Having anything to do with the murder weapon ties me into the killing, and that's not going to happen."

"Ah, come on, Earl! I've wiped all the prints off it. Things like that never bothered you before! What's your problem?"

A fleeting image of Addie's face raced through his mind. "Nothing!" he declared. "Request number two?"

"I need to have sex with you."

"What?"

"Do I have to repeat it?"

"Please don't! What in the world are you up to now?"

"I've already told you that Steve won't have sex with me anymore. Since I need to be pregnant to keep him, I really thought you'd jump at the chance to help me."

A wave of revulsion swept over him. So that's why she'd brought him to this isolated smelly spot.

"You are out of your mind, Ellen! There's no way in hell I'm having sex with you! And another thing, I'm not getting rid of Addie."

Ellen's eyes went wild.

"Hold on, now. Before you explode, you have to know that getting rid of her would not make Steve love you. In fact, he would be so upset that he wouldn't give you the time of day. You have to believe me when I say that's what would happen."

"What am I going to do then? Right now is my fertile time and I can't wait another month." She threatened to tear up again.

"Let me keep Addie away from Steve. You just concentrate on making yourself lovable for Steve. Okay?"

She nodded, gave one last sniff, and then pointed to the bag. "Earl, please say you'll get rid of these things!"

He thought for a moment. If he were the only one who knew where the jacket and bat were, he would forever have a bargaining chip to hold over Ellen if things went south in the future.

Giving a slight nod of the head, he agreed. "You could have at least brought me a shovel, but leave the bag with me and I'll take care of it."

Evelyn Allen Harper

She slid across the seat and kissed him on the cheek. "I knew I could count on you! Thank you, Earl. And since I see that you're wearing rubber gloves, I take it that I'm sitting in a stolen car?"

"What else? I have no money to rent one. You know the drill, wipe off any place you touched; don't forget the outside, too."

She was heading for her car when he rolled down the window and called to her. "What are you going to do about the pregnancy thing?"

Turning around, she yelled back, "I'm off to Joe's Bar and Grill. I'm betting I'll find someone there. It should have been you, though."

Grabbing the bag, he crawled over the fence to the dump, found the only tree on the site, and with a stick, scratched a shallow hole.

Chapter 29

Addie's rigid body dared any of her fellow workers to crack a joke about her boss's reprimand. All that fuss over thirty seconds?

An instant message appeared on her screen; it was a summons to his office.

What now?

Fleeting memories from her school days were racing through her head. The same feeling of dread that she'd had as a kid standing outside the principal's office was now making her adult knees weak. Back then, the big fear was that the principal would share her transgression with her parents; the big fear now was the loss of her job.

A surprisingly warm voice answered her timid knock on his door. "Please come in, Addie."

The soft sound of his voice puzzled her; that was not the voice of someone who was angry. Taking a deep breath, she squared her shoulders and opened the door.

Mr. Lawson motioned for her to sit. Addie sat, crossed her feet, clasped her hands in her lap, and waited.

He kept his eyes down for a moment before he lifted them to look at her. The gentleness of his appearance startled her.

Speaking softly he said, "Addie, I'm so sorry I did that."

Her mouth dropped open.

When she didn't say anything, he continued. "I'd just had a very upsetting thing happen at lunch, and I apologize for taking it out on you. You didn't deserve that kind of treatment."

Relieved, she smiled and relaxed. "I accept your apology, and I'm sorry you had a bad lunch."

Dare he ask who her companion was? "And you, Addie? Did you have a good lunch?"

Her face lit up, and her eyes were shining when she answered, "It was a *wonderful* lunch!"

That's what he was afraid of.

"Thanks for accepting my apology," he said as he ushered her out. "I'm sorry that it happened."

*****

Addie sat at her desk and pondered over what had just occurred. Something bad had happened to him at lunch. Maybe he'd gotten orders from the owner to shut down the magazine. To her, that would be the same as being fired; she wouldn't have a job.

Feeling helpless because she had no say in the matter, she was wondering what she could do to help sell more magazines when she opened her bottom drawer and saw Worried's envelope that had the return address in the left-hand corner. Would the reader of *Your World* be interested in her tracking down recipients to find out if Dr. Ask-Me-Anything's advice had helped? Since her job was to treat their problem with nothing but caustic nonsense, their response might make a very amusing addition to her column.

Excited by the idea, she was heading for Mr. Lawson's office when she stopped. Maybe the recipients didn't want a public follow-up. And come to think about it, Worried was the only one whose envelope had a return address on it.

Feeling like a deflated balloon, she turned around and went back to her desk, trying to accept the fact that she'd never know if Worried took her advice.

She tucked Worried's letter back into her bottom desk drawer.

It was 5:45, time to collect her things because at the stroke of 6:00, she planned on being on the elevator heading down to the main floor where Earl would be waiting for her. Just thinking about Earl's promise of cuddling by the fireplace sent chills up and down her spine. If she had her way, this night was going to be the start of something big…really big.

Never before had time moved so slowly. What Addie was feeling was hard to explain because she'd never felt it before. Mixed in with excitement was another nameless element that was putting a goofy grin on her face. Ever since lunch, her world seemed different. Were the colors really brighter, or were her eyes playing tricks on her? Looking around, she glanced at her boss. Even Mr. Law…Jim was looking good, for a boss. Funny, it was because he was her boss that she had never really looked at him that way, but he really was an attractive man.

Five minutes had passed since the last time she'd looked at the clock. Just thinking about Earl made her heart race. If only she'd picked a more attractive outfit this morning, but she hadn't, and there was nothing she could do about it now. Three times she had gone to the restroom and tried to do something exotic with her hair and make-up, but when the end result had her looking like a street-walker, she scrubbed her face and unpinned her hair.

The second hand on the clock was sweeping its way to twelve. Finally! Feeling like a runner waiting for the starting gun to go off, she jumped when she heard her boss ask, "Addie, could I buy you a drink?"

All the air went out of her lungs. She wanted to scream at him to get out of her way because at the end of her elevator ride the most devastatingly handsome man in the whole world was waiting for her.

She bit her tongue and took a deep breath. This was the boss who gave her a job that earned her the money that paid her bills.

"Oh, hello, Jim," she forced a smiled. "Could I ask for a rain check on that drink? I do have other plans."

He swallowed hard; rejection stung. "Rain check it is."

"Thank you."

"Looks like you're ready to leave."

"I am," she smiled up at him, hoping her refusal wasn't going to cause trouble.

"So am I," he replied. "Shall we take the elevator down together?"

"Sure," Addie said pressing the call button, because there was nothing else she could say. When the elevator arrived they stepped in together and stood awkwardly to either side, not looking at one another. She wasn't sure of Jim's intentions, but she was sure it was beginning to cross the line of purely professional.

This was wrong in so many ways. She didn't really want her boss to see her walk off with Earl, and she didn't want Earl to get the wrong idea when he saw her getting off the elevator with a truly good-looking guy.

Neither one of them said a word on the trip down from the sixth floor. When the door opened, Earl was right there waiting for her with a rose in his hand.

Addie blushed, waved a quick goodbye to Jim and took Earl's extended hand.

*****

Jim watched Addie walk off holding the hand of the guy who'd been her lunch date. Now he really needed a drink. Just thinking of all the ways he'd screwed up with Addie was making him physically ill. She said she'd forgiven him for embarrassing her about being just half a minute late, but had she?

The strong need for alcohol hit him hard. The closest place he could think of was Joe's Bar and Grill.

Chapter 30

Earl's eyes followed the elevator's progress as it made its way down from the sixth floor. He was still breathing hard from the effort to be on time.

Ordering the restaurant food had been a brilliant idea and all was on schedule when he entered the house he'd been living in since getting out of prison. It was really Ellen's house, one that she'd inherited from her parents but didn't need any more since her marriage to Steve.

Earl stood with his arms loaded with a five-course meal for two from the most expensive restaurant in town and viewed the house through Addie's eyes. Clutter was everywhere. Dropped socks, shoes, shirts, newspapers, coffee cups and a wet towel from his last shower were on the floor. In the kitchen, dirty dishes filled the sink, and pots and pans on the stove were caked with dried food.

He had a decision to make. He could tell Addie that there had been a change of plans and there would be no home-cooked meal and no cuddling by the fire, or he could roll up his sleeves and start cleaning. Not only had he spent a small fortune on the food, it smelled so good he couldn't stand the thought of not eating it.

Picking up all the dirty clothes, he ran to the laundry room, tossed them into the washer, and before slamming the door, grabbed an empty clothes basket which was soon filled with the rest of the litter.

The bathroom was a nightmare; he hadn't cleaned it in all the time that he'd lived here. Sweat was running down his cheeks even before he tackled the kitchen.

Waves of exhaustion were sweeping over him by the time he'd cleaned the kitchen. Glancing at the time, he was shocked to see how late it was. It had been all too easy to say, "Tonight I'll even throw in a home-cooked dinner before story time." What was he thinking? Now he had to find dishes to fill with the restaurant food to make it look as if he had cooked it himself.

After setting the table for two, he noticed the dust on the furniture and the dirt on the carpet. Vacuuming was the last thing he did before he stepped into the shower.

Addie stood in Earl's kitchen and her whole body was tingling; never before had she felt such excitement just being with a man. What she'd experienced with Steve paled in comparison. Thank God he'd married Ellen!

Did she really mean that? She remembered how excited she'd been when she thought Steve was going to propose, but here she was, just a short time later, thanking God that he'd married someone else. Go figure.

Earl had prepared a feast.

He was trying to stifle a yawn when Addie exclaimed, "My goodness, Earl! You must have cooked all day."

The yawn won.

After recovering, he waved his hand, rolled his watery blue eyes, and claimed, "It's nothing special."

When she started to clear the table after they'd eaten, he wrapped his arms around her, kissed her on the neck, and ushered her onto the couch in front of the fireplace.

"Forget the dishes. I'll take care of them tomorrow. You just sit here while I make the fire. Cuddling and story time coming up!"

As she watched him load the fireplace with logs, she had no idea that the bulging muscled arms that were making her heart beat faster were the product of the prison's gym. If she had her way, those arms were going to hold her while they cuddled by the fire. At first she had feared that tonight things might get out of control, but now she feared that maybe he'd be too much of a gentleman and things wouldn't get out of control. It shocked her to realize how much she wanted those lips to kiss her. Anticipation built, and with it came the realization that if he didn't make the first romantic move, then she would.

The fire was burning brightly when Earl came back from the kitchen with two glasses of wine, sat down beside her on the couch and yawned.

Addie slid closer to him. "Story time?" she asked softly.

Earl leaned his head back and closed his eyes. "What?"

Her voice was hoarse with desire. "You promised me cuddling and a story, Earl."

Nothing happened.

"Earl?"

Sweet Adeline

His tipped wine glass landed in her lap as his long body slid until it was stretched out on the couch. Earl had fallen asleep, and to add insult to injury, he was snoring.

A disappointed Addie sopped up the spilled wine on her dress with a paper towel. Her car was back at work and Earl was fast asleep.

She called a cab.

Chapter 31

It was Happy Hour at Joe's Bar and Grill. Jim Lawson stood for a moment, waiting for his eyes to adjust to the dim lighting. Two- dollar drafts and three-dollar cocktails for the next two hours – perfect.

Every seat around the bar was occupied and most of the tables were full. He was about to turn around and leave when one man at the bar held up his hand, signaling to the bartender that he wanted to settle his bill.

Jim claimed the warm seat before anyone else grabbed it and waited for the bartender to take his order.

"Whisky sour, minus the sour, no ice," he told the man, "and keep them coming."

There wasn't enough alcohol in the world to make him forget that he'd embarrassed Addie in front of her co-workers for being a measly thirty seconds late. The way she'd emphasized his formal name spoke volumes; she'd probably never call him Jim again. And to top it off, now she was out with that good-looking guy who was clever enough to show up with just one rose in his hand. That one rose was much more impressive than two dozen would have been.

The man next to him got up, paid his bill and looked at Jim, "You downed that drink in thirty-seconds," he chuckled.

Jim just shrugged.

By the bottom of the third drink, he'd admitted to himself that if Addie made choices based on looks alone, the outrageously handsome guy would win. By the fourth drink, he had her married to the guy. By the fifth drink, he imagined how he would feel if her handsome husband moved her to another state and he'd never, ever see her again. That thought sent him into uncontrolled sobbing. Until a hand landed on his shoulder, he had been so busy mopping up the tears that he hadn't noticed that the empty seat beside him was now occupied.

"Someone die?" a woman asked in a soft voice.

"What?" He hadn't realized how drunk he was until he swung around to see who had interrupted his pity-party. Losing his balance, he grabbed at the nearest stable thing to make the world stop spinning.

"Whoa!" the woman yelled as the man she was sitting beside threw his arms around her and hung on. Struggling to keep them both on their seats, she tried to pry his arms from around her. The more she pulled, the harder he gripped.

"None of them shenanigans in my bar," the bartender snarled. "Pay your bill and get the hell out!"

"B...but," the woman started to protest.

"You heard me! There's no making out at my bar. Either you two leave on your own or I can have the bouncer escort you out the door."

Muttering under her breath, the woman threw money onto the bar, settled the man on his unsteady feet, and headed for the door.

Jim was drunk. His whole world was spinning but he wasn't crying anymore. Getting kicked out of a bar was kinda funny. The more he thought about it, the funnier it became. Laughing, he slid out of the woman's grasp, and when he found himself sitting on his butt in the middle of the parking lot, he threw his head back and howled.

When the laughter turned to giggles and the giggles turned to hiccups, the woman pulled him to his feet and patiently urged him along to her car.

Ellen grinned. Finding a man to father her baby had been almost too easy.

Chapter 32

Jeb Linden squirmed, scratched and rubbed the parts of his body that were complaining about the coarse material of his jail-issued clothing. Whoever did the laundry in this place should ask Cindy how she makes everything she washes so soft.

Cindy.

He could forget about it for a dozen seconds, but reality was always there waiting to punch him in the stomach. Sometimes, it hit so hard his whole body curled in on itself.

He felt helpless. His court-appointed attorney's interest wasn't really on him, a man who was being accused of an ordinary domestic-related murder, but on defending a down-and-out former two-bit actor who was charged with killing a fellow boardinghouse tenant.

To Jeb, it felt as if he were in solitary confinement most of the time. There was no one else around and except for the guard who brought his meals and then took away the empty dishes; his days were long and lonely. The actor had been a ray of sunshine for the few hours he had been locked up, but that ended when a fan bailed him out.

Why was he still in jail? A good lawyer would have kept him from going to jail in the first place. He didn't know too much about legal matters, but being kept in jail because of a bad alibi just didn't sound reasonable. But his jacket had been found near the murder scene, and he had been walking in the area.

The only thing the police didn't have was a motive. A good lawyer would have objected to the laughter that erupted when he answered, "The dog did it," to why his jacket was ripped. There was even more laughter when a voice called out, "Did the dog eat your homework, too?" He had to admit that his story of how the dog had gotten hold of his jacket sounded made-up, but it was the truth.

With nothing else to do but sleep, he had just dozed off when chatter from the front office woke him. Excited voices meant something unexpected had happened. He listened for a bit but when no one came down the hall, he closed his eyes and went back to sleep.

Sweet Adeline
*****

"Who the hell is Dr. Ask-Me-Anything?" was the question that had the front office in an uproar. Sgt. Green, who had just returned from a warranted search of Jeb Linden's home, waved the envelope that was causing the loud chatter. It had just been one of many items that the mailman had deposited in Jeb's mailbox.

"Did Dr. Ask-Me-Anything include a return address?" an officer asked.

Sgt. Green shook his head. "No address, just the name. Whoever addressed the envelope has a fancy style of writing. Oh, the postmark is ours, so the good doctor is probably a local female. Wonder who Dr. Ask-Me-Anything really is."

Miss Wade, the secretary in the front office, had one ear tuned to the chatter coming from the front office. "Get on the Internet," she called out. "Look up the magazine, *Your World.*"

Within minutes, Sgt. Green had the newest issue of the magazine on his computer screen. Finding the Dr. Ask-Me-Anything column was easy. The office was silent as each officer read the inquiry and the Doctor's answer over Sgt. Green's shoulder.

"The motive we've been looking for just might be inside that envelope. Can we open it?" one officer exclaimed.

Sgt. Green shook his head. "Not without some legal advice. Who's Jeb's lawyer?"

Miss Wade called from her office, "Bob Hilton, and I have his phone number."

Bob Hilton, Esq., had volunteered his services as the actor's attorney because the drunk couldn't afford to hire one for himself. He was basking in the limelight of his fifteen minutes of fame even knowing he would lose in court. Defending Jeb paled in comparison.

Bob's voice, when he answered his phone, was slurred and hard to hear over the background noise.

"Bob, this is Sgt. Joe Green. I'm calling about one of your clients, Jeb Linden."

"Jeb?" A pause, and then, "Oh, yes. I remember now. Killed his wife, didn't he?"

Sgt. Green made a face; the lawyer was obviously drunk. Jeb didn't have a chance with this loser as his defender.

"Could you answer a legal question?"

Bob was too busy laughing at something to even hear the question.

"Bob?"

"Oh, you still there?"

"Where are you?" a suspicious Sgt. Green asked.

"Uh, I'm at Joe's Bar and Grill. My client is entertaining some old friends from his Hollywood days. You won't recognize them because they were all character actors, but you'll see us all in tomorrow's paper!"

"Bob, could I get you to think about a legal question?"

"That's what I get the big money for," he giggled. "What's the question?"

"While doing a warranted search, do the police have the right to open a letter that was left in the mailbox?"

Bob cleared his throat and sobered up. "The Fourth Amendment says they can't, but with probable cause, a judge can issue a proper warrant if he feels that the letter has some connection to the case."

"Thank yo—"

Bob had turned off his phone.

When Sgt. Green repeated what Bob had told him, the big question was what could be the probable cause that would convince a judge to issue such a warrant. Amid the heated conversation, one voice rose above the rest.

"All we have to do is watch Jeb's reaction when he sees Dr. Ask-Me-Anything's name in the return address."

"Sounds too easy," one officer muttered.

"You have a better idea?"

*****

Jeb's face was radiant, his smile was wide, and his eyes were full of love as he stood at the front of the church and watched Cindy walk toward him. Dressed in pure white, she made a stunning bride. Hell, she was just as stunning in jeans…and she was going to marry him. He was about to pinch himself to make sure this was really happening when voices from the wedding party interrupted the ceremony.

"Jeb, wake up!"

Why was Charles wrecking his wedding? His best man was yelling in a voice that didn't sound like him at all.

"Wake up!"

Sweet Adeline

The wedding scene faded away as Jeb's eyes slowly opened. He wasn't dressed in a tux, his Cindy was dead and he was in jail. Could things get any worse? That's when he noticed that several uniformed men were looking through the bars at him. His stomach sank; his gut feeling told him that things could get worse.

He sat up, ran his fingers through his hair, and tried to get the dream out of his head. It had been so real!

Sgt. Green had an envelope in his hand. "Jeb, we're just delivering the mail."

"Oh? I have mail? Someone sent me a letter here?"

"No, it was delivered to your home."

Jeb looked startled. "You went to my house? Did you go in?"

"Yes, we did."

"What right do you have to go into my home?" Jeb was getting upset.

"Every right; you're a suspect in a murder," one of the officers said. Jeb's face flinched as if he'd been hit.

"We had a warrant," Sgt. Green said, a bit softer.

Jeb's shoulders drooped. "You didn't find anything, did you?" When no one answered him, he continued, "That's because there's nothing to find. Whatever happened to 'innocent until proven guilty'? How many times do I have to tell you that I loved my wife and I sure as hell didn't kill her? The killer is out there somewhere laughing at you while I'm in here. That bastard could be hurting other people and you just stand here thinking because I'm her husband, that I," Jeb choked on a sob, "I didn't hurt my wife."

Sgt. Green felt a pang of sympathy for the man sitting on the cot. From the beginning, he'd thought Jeb was innocent. His initial reaction to the news that his wife was dead had been no act; Jeb had been truly devastated. He had pushed to look elsewhere for the real killer, but that changed when he found Jeb's jacket near the murder scene. Jeb's evening stroll hadn't helped, and now the letter. A good lawyer might be able to get him out of this, but he didn't have a good lawyer.

Ignoring the remark, he stepped close to the bars. "Here's your letter, Jeb."

Jeb threw his legs over the edge of his cot, stood up, reached out his arm, and took the letter.

This was it. The officers waited. What Jeb did when his eyes landed on the top left-hand part of the envelope and saw Dr. Ask-Me-Anything's name would determine if the envelope contained something that would meet the criteria for probable cause.

Jeb's heart threatened to stop when he saw Dr. Ask-Me-Anything's name. He *had* used one of Cindy's stamped envelopes when he sent that stupid advice request to *Your World* magazine. To the police, that inquiry would give them the motive they were looking for.

As the officers watched, the expression on Jeb's face changed. His eyes widened, he seemed to shrink before their eyes, and his hand trembled. It didn't matter what was inside the envelope; just the fact that there was one was damning evidence.

Knowing all hope was lost, he gave a cry of anguish and threw himself onto his cot. Putting the pillow over his head to smother the sounds of his sobs, he cried until there were no tears left.

Too bad his court-appointed lawyer was such a loser. It didn't help that he remembered reading the statistics about how many more people who use them end up in jail compared to those who were able to hire their own lawyer, guilty or not. He and Cindy had lived from paycheck to paycheck with nothing left to put into a savings account.

Why wouldn't anyone tell him about Cindy? Was his wife on some slab in cold storage at the morgue? The very thought sent him into more body-wracking sobs.

If only he had someone to talk to…someone who believed him when he swore that he hadn't killed her.

Dark waves of desperation and hopelessness were the only companions in his isolated existence.

*****

Miss Wade, the secretary in the front office, had one ear tuned to the chatter coming from the officers and one ear tuned to the fax machine. She was waiting on a fax from city hall pertaining to their prisoner, Jeb Linden. So far, the man had a clean record, not even a parking ticket.

It had taken forever, but finally the fax machine came to life. Grabbing the paper that the machine spit out, she was disgusted to see that what had been sent to her was not about Jeb Linden. The

Sweet Adeline

new person in charge of records had goofed again. The job paid so little, no intelligent person ever filled the position.

"That Linden's report?" Sgt. Green asked her.

Miss Wade shook her head, "Nope, a marriage certificate for some couple; that numbskull over there has fewer brains than a parakeet. I asked for information about Jeb Linden and what do I get? A marriage certificate!"

"For Jeb and Cindy?"

"Nope, Albert Richard Linder and Ellen Joyce Short – hope they don't need this."

"That office is a joke. Let me know if anything comes over about Jeb. I'm sure Bob will want it when he's sober," Sgt. Green said, shaking his head.

Nodding, Miss Wade balled up the useless fax and aimed for the wastebasket.

Chapter 33

The noise of something being dropped on the floor of the bathroom roused Steve in the middle of a dream. It had been a nice one and he hated to leave it, knowing that if he didn't grab it immediately the dream would slide into oblivion. At this point in his life, the dream had to be better than reality; anything would be better than reality. Reality was in the bathroom making funny noises. Reality's name was Ellen. At least Reality wasn't in bed trying to coax him into having sex. That wasn't going to happen because his body hadn't risen to the occasion since the day she announced that she was off the pill.

Steve dug back into the covers, wishing he didn't have to wake up and face the nightmare his life had become. It disgusted him when he faced the truth; he had married a memory. Damn that reunion! All it had taken was one look at the girl who had smashed his heart and the old memories turned his head into mush. If only he could stop his life at that point and make a different decision! A sensible Steve would not have rushed off to a Justice of the Peace with a woman he hadn't seen in years. A sensible Steve would never have ended up married to a woman he didn't even like. What if he hadn't gone to the reunion? What if...

Playing the "what if?" game never changed anything. The only way out of the mess he had made of his life was to divorce Ellen and get back with Addie. She might claim that she was through with him, but minds can be changed.

Now if Ellen would knock off the noise in the bathroom, he had thirty minutes to sleep before the alarm went off.

*****

Ellen held the pregnancy test in shaky hands. This was it. If that guy in the bar hadn't gotten her pregnant, her only chance to hold Steve was gone. If she were pregnant now, the child could be passed off as Steve's.

While waiting for the stick to change colors, she prayed while pacing back and forth. Steve was her one chance to make something of her life. If she lost him, then she'd be back with Earl pulling off deals that usually ended in jail time.

Sweet Adeline

The stick was changing....

"Yes! Yes!" she cried.

Half asleep, the noise startled Steve and his eyes flew open. Why would Ellen be shouting "Yes! Yes!" at six o'clock in the morning? Crazy woman! He sighed in resignation, threw off the covers, and crawled out of bed.

"Ellen," he called, "what the hell is going on in there?"

Ellen froze with the colored stick in her hand. There was a moment of panic when she realized that her whole future depended on her coming up with a believable reason for her outburst.

Think! Think!

Then it hit her. Lately she'd noticed that her new husband really didn't listen to her lengthy stories. Oh, he'd nod his head every once in a while but she could tell he wasn't interested.

Taking a deep breath, she called back, "Oh Sweetie, did I wake you? I'm so sorry! But Sherri...you've gotta remember Sherri. She was in our chemistry class, sat right behind you? Well, she called from Europe and you and I know that the girl never was good at math! She figured the time difference wrong, which is not surprising. She said to say hi to my new husband, so Hi Stevie baby! She met someone in Italy and they are going to get married! Isn't that a blast? We never thought anyone would ever marry her considering she isn't the prettiest peach in the basket, but it sounds like she found someone who doesn't mind her mustache and crossed eyes. Isn't that wonderful? She just had to call and tell me the good news. And get this! She wants me to be in her wedding. How am I going to get out of that? I had to say yes, I really did, but I'm not going to do it. I don't want to be in the wedding party of a crossed-eyed mustached bride!" Ellen stopped for breath and listened. Steve was snoring.

101

Chapter 34

Mike looked at the wall clock and noted the time. After he cleaned the front office, he was through for the night. Miss Wade always kept this room uncluttered, not like some of the other offices. He didn't know her, but since she had a plaque on her desk with her name on it, he felt as if he did.

The vibration of his phone startled him. Who would be calling at midnight?

"Hello?"

"Mike, it's your mother."

He inwardly groaned. Ever since his dad died six months ago she'd become extremely clingy.

"Yes?"

"I need you to stop at the all-night store and pick up some things for me."

"Can't it wait 'til tomorrow?"

"No. My book club meeting is tomorrow and I'm supposed to bring a dessert."

Mike sighed. "Okay, I'll do it. What am I supposed to buy?"

"You need to write it down. The last time you tried to use your memory, you forgot two things."

"This would be a lot easier if you learned how to send a text message, Mom."

"It would be easier if you just wrote it down and didn't argue with me, Michael."

"Mom, I can't go through someone's desk and look for paper and pen! How many things are there?"

"More than you can remember. Use your head, Son! Look in the waste basket."

One look at the basket told Mike he wasn't going to find a usable piece of paper there; a discarded cup of coffee had soaked everything. He could hear his impatient mother breathing heavily.

"Well?" she asked.

"I'm having trouble finding paper…oh, wait a minute." He had just spied something on the floor. Picking it up, he smoothed out the crumpled piece of paper, and found a pen.

Sweet Adeline

"Okay, Mom. I'm ready. What do you need?"

*****

Two o'clock in the morning found Mike in the all-night store roaming up and down the aisles trying to find the items for his mom's dessert. His spelling was atrocious and his handwriting was almost unreadable but knowing what he'd be in for if he arrived home without the things on the list, he shopped on.

Jack, the clerk, was working with another customer but that didn't keep him from noticing that Mike was getting more and more frustrated. Finishing up with the customer, Jack reached into the recycle box and grabbed scraps of paper that he scrunched up and stuffed between the two bottles of wine so they wouldn't clang together.

"Have a good night, Bill," Jack said to his departing customer.

"Thanks, Jack."

Jack called out to Mike when he noticed that his shopping cart was still empty. "Can I help you find something? You've been wandering in here for a while."

"You'd do that?" Mike asked relieved.

Jack nodded at him, "Do it all the time."

"Thanks a lot, Jack, I really appreciate it. You know how my mother can be." Holding out the list, he added sheepishly, "Sorry about the spelling and the handwriting,"

"I'll figure it out," Jack said.

The door of the store opened, and a customer walked in. After looking around, he gestured toward the row of bottles marked "Buy One, Get One Free."

"Is this sale for all wines?" he called over to Jack.

Jack shook his head, "No, just the red!"

Turning to Mike, Jack said, "You're all set. I found everything on the list. Meet me at the register and I'll check you out. Oh, here's your list."

"Thanks again, Jack!"

On his way to the door, Mike tossed the list into the recycle box.

"Anytime, Mike." Jack waved to the boy and turned to ring up the man's two bottles of red.

"Hot date?" Jack laughed.

*****

Evelyn Allen Harper

It was late, but since that was the best time to ditch a stolen car, Earl was driving around looking for an opportunity. What it would be, he had no idea; he would recognize it when he saw it.

He was passing an all-night store when he noticed a car pulling out of a parking place. As he watched, the car hesitated and then pulled back in. When the driver stepped out of the still-running car and reentered the store, Earl saw his opportunity. Since he had already removed the bike rack off the top of the car and there were no fingerprints to wipe off, he quickly parked it, left the keys in the ignition, and within seconds, he was driving off in another stolen vehicle.

Inside the store, Jack looked up as his last customer rushed back through the door.

"Can't believe I forgot my credit card, I tell ya. My wife says I'd forget my head if it weren't hooked on!" the man laughed. Jack nodded and was about to hand him his card when he glanced out the window.

"Hey, Buddy! I think someone just drove off with your car!"

Chapter 35

Addie plastered a pleasant look on her face trying to hide the pain of last night's disappointment. What should have been the beginning of something huge had turned into nothing more than a lonely taxi ride home. To top it off, the wine had ruined her dress. Her first thought was to throw it away, but she changed her mind. She would keep it as a reminder not to set her expectations too high.

What was she supposed to do now? They hadn't exchanged telephone numbers, so calling him was out. She did know where he lived, though. Conflicting thoughts flew through her head. He'd seemed so interested, so why had the evening ended the way it had? Wait a minute. He could have that sickness that makes you go to sleep even if you don't want to. One of her high school teachers had asked her to be a watchdog and wake her up if she had her head down on her desk when a visitor or the principal were about to come into the room. Narcolepsy. Yes, that was the name of it. If that were the case, she should sympathize with Earl and not be angry. On the other hand…

Her door opened and her boss stood in the doorway holding a basket of flowers so big he had to stand sideways.

"Mr. Lawson!" Addie gasped. "You shouldn't have! Really, this is—"

"No, Addie, these are not from me. You'll have to read the card."

"My goodness! Who would send me something like this?" Addie was looking around, trying to find a place in her small office to put the monstrosity. "I guess you're going to have to set it on the floor."

The heavy basket hit the floor with a thud. "Wow!" he exclaimed. "Somewhere in this town there's an empty greenhouse!"

"How am I supposed to find the card in the middle of…of all that?"

He handed her an envelope. "The card isn't in the arrangement."

"Thanks goodness for that!"

He watched her face as she opened the envelope and read the card. Whoever had sent the flowers had the ability to make Addie's whole body respond. Her shoulders relaxed, her face softened, and she grinned.

"Well?" he asked.

"Uh." Addie decided to lie. "It just says 'From a secret admirer.'"

"Really?" his eyebrows shot up.

"Really."

The truth hit him with a gut-punch; no secret admirer had sent the flowers. Knowing who had, the sweet aroma of the flowers turned into a funeral stench.

Addie noticed her boss's face had changed color. "You all right?" she asked.

He swallowed the bile that was pushing its way up his throat. "I just need some fresh air," he muttered as he rushed out of the room.

Hiding inside the bathroom stall, Jim fought the rising nausea. How could he compete with someone who was not only good-looking but was also financially able to spend a small fortune on flowers?

*****

"You damned-sticky-fingered-scum!" Earl held the phone away from his ear. "Did you really think you were going to get away with it?"

"Ah, come on, Ellen," he whined. "How's a man going to woo a princess if he doesn't have any money?"

"Does the word 'job' give you an idea?"

"There really aren't a lot of employers lining up to hire an ex-con. And don't act like you don't know it, so lighten up!"

After a moment of silence, she replied, "I know that. But I want that credit card back before you get any more bright ideas. It's bad enough that I'm giving you spending money from my grocery allowance, but I don't know how I'm going to explain the charge of a five-course dinner for two and a shit-load of flowers."

"Should be a snap for you, Babe. I've seen you get out of worse situations than this. But tell me, how are things on the home front now that you don't have the pregnancy card to play?"

Sweet Adeline

Ellen fell silent. The secret that the guy she'd picked up at the bar had fathered a child was too big to share with anyone. "I made a mistake when I told you I wasn't pregnant."

"Wait a minute. You're telling me that when you pulled that scene at the dump you were already pregnant?"

"Yeah. Didn't I just tell you that I made a mistake?"

"The last thing you said when you left me at the dump was that you were heading for Joe's to find someone to fuck because it was your fertile period."

"Listen to me carefully. I never went to Joe's, and you better never say that I did!"

Earl snorted. "And you're a dirty little liar, Ellen. I know very well that you did go to Joe's. And now, how clean are you? Are you sure you didn't get more than just stud service at Joe's? Steve's not going to like it if you brought something home with you…besides a baby."

"Earl, just keep your filthy mouth shut! Do you hear me? It's going to be hard enough to pull this off because everything about this baby will be a month behind schedule."

Earl was laughing when she hung up on him.

Chapter 36

It was amazing that a few words written on a card could turn a miserable day into a bright and sunny one. Holding the card close to her heart, her face beamed until the sudden departure of her boss brought her back to reality. Suspecting that Mr. Law...Jim....had feelings for her made her feel uneasy. She felt bad for him, but what could she do about it? He was just her boss, for heaven's sake!

Earl had written an apology for falling asleep, explaining that earlier in the day he'd worn himself out helping a recently widowed old woman move into a retirement home. It pleased her to know that Earl had a kind heart, but it was the very last sentence that made her the happiest. He asked for a second chance.

It was almost noon when she noticed two uniformed police officers talking to Mr. Lawson. Butterflies danced in her stomach when he pointed his finger in her direction. The butterflies were in full flight by the time the cops reached her office.

The two of them entered and abruptly stopped at the sight and smell of the huge mound of flowers.

One of the officers spoke softly to his buddy. "Some poor dude bought his way out of hot water!"

"Wow!" the other man whispered back. "He must have really messed up! That had to set him back a penny or two!"

Addie cleared her throat. "May I help you?"

The officers turned around and faced her.

"We understand that you are Dr. Ask-Me-Anything."

She looked surprised. "Did Mr. Lawson tell you that?"

They nodded.

"I was told my identity was to remain anonymous. Why did he tell you?"

"We won't reveal that it's you, but we're in the middle of a murder investigation. We need to ask you some questions."

"Murder? Oh, no! Have I done something wrong?"

"No, no. We just need the letter you received from Worried in the Suburbs, you know, the one that you answered in your magazine column."

Sweet Adeline

"And why do you need it?"

"That's police business, Miss Parker."

"But—"

"It would be best if you'd cooperate with us. If not, we'll come back with a warrant."

"May I have a moment to speak to Mr. Lawson?"

"Go right ahead."

Addie left her office and confronted him.

"Did they tell you what they want me to do?" she asked.

He nodded. "You really don't have a choice. One way or another, they'll get what they want. They know that Jeb wrote the request because the police have the follow-up letter you sent him. They just want the original for evidence."

"It sounds like Jeb is in trouble."

"He is. He's being accused of killing his wife."

Addie gasped. The only way he could be connected to Dr. Ask-Me-Anything was through that stupid follow-up letter. Her knees threatened to collapse. Because of her, a man might spend the rest of his life in prison even if he didn't do it. Or maybe her response was the reason he killed her. Maybe he had confronted his wife, just like she had suggested, and found out that she was cheating. Horrified, Addie stared at Jim.

"So I don't have a choice? I have to give it to them?"

"That's right."

Addie hung her head. "He sounded like such a nice man who just loved his wife and didn't understand what was going on. But he did admit to stalking her, and he did say he couldn't stand the thought of another man touching her. Mr. Lawson, that letter will condemn Jeb, whether he did it or not." She burst into tears. "Oh, God! I'm the one who told him to confront her!"

Recognizing an opportunity when he saw one, Jim pulled the sobbing Addie into his arms. "Addie, crying won't help because what's done is done. It's out of our hands now."

She was still sobbing on his shoulder when the police left with the original envelope, the one Jeb's wife had so lovingly supplied with the stamp and the return address in the upper left-hand corner.

Chapter 37

Jeb stared at his court-appointed lawyer who had just uttered words that, if true, would put him behind bars for the rest of his life.

"Don't look at me like that, Jeb," Bob Hilton snapped while holding up the issue of *Your World*. "I didn't write those words, you did."

"I know it sounds bad, but I never threatened to kill her! I would never hurt her!"

"You might as well have. Stating that you couldn't stand the thought of some other man touching your wife shows that you could be angry enough to kill her if you found out that there was another man."

"B…but..!"

"'Buts' don't stand a chance in court. You also admit stalking her. That's bad business, Jeb."

"But I didn't kill her!" Jeb was at the end of holding back tears.

"Tears don't help either, big guy."

Jeb mopped his face. "Aren't lawyers supposed to believe their clients? It doesn't even sound like you're trying to get me out of this mess."

Bob shrugged. "What do I have to work with?"

"Find the murder weapon! Find the real killer, because it sure isn't me! How does it make you feel knowing that the real killer is out there laughing his head off?"

With an irritatingly smug look on his face, Bob replied, "Oh, I don't really believe that's happening."

Jeb studied his lawyer with nothing but disgust in his eyes. "Guard!" he yelled. "I want to go back to my cell."

*****

Ellen kept looking into her rearview mirror. The stolen car had different license plates, a pretend bike rack on its top, and a decal on its bumper proclaiming that the driver's child was an honor student at West Junior High, but it was still a stolen car. Driving with rubber gloves on didn't bother her; she'd done it before. For

Sweet Adeline

years, "No prints left behind" had been one of Earl's favorite sayings.

Not having a car of her own really bugged her. Today had been her appointment with the doctor to validate her pregnancy. Steve hadn't asked why she needed the car; he had just assured her that she could have it. But an emergency had come up at work, and even though he'd left a note of apology for her to read when she got up this morning, it hadn't solved the car problem. That's where Earl had come into the picture, and that's why she was driving a stolen car and looking into the rearview mirror.

The appointment lasted all of thirty minutes, minus all the paperwork. "There it is," the doctor said pointing to a tiny dot on the screen. "Congratulations! You're going to be a mother."

Ellen beamed.

"Do you want me to print out a picture?" she asked.

Ellen nodded enthusiastically.

While Ellen studied the dot that was going to bind Steve in their marriage, the doctor prattled on about prenatal vitamins and the importance of regular check-ups. "Feel free to bring your husband with you when you come."

"I will do that!" Ellen replied to the doctor, but in her mind she was thinking, "Over my dead body."

*****

Ellen couldn't keep the smile off her face on her way home. Yes, she was pregnant! Steve was going to be shocked at dinner tonight. Should she tell him before the meal, or after? Should they have wine to toast the occasion? Wait a minute. Pregnant women aren't supposed to drink wine so no, there would be no toast to the happy event. The words "happy event" made her pause. She knew very well that the news would not be a happy event for Steve. She'd overheard a phone conversation the other night when he was sure she was asleep. The word "divorce" had been uttered. Thank God the guy at Joe's had been willing and able! Come to think about it, he was good looking, too. Tall, dark and handsome really fit his description. And his eyes! They were so dark they almost looked black. Wonder what his name was?

Since she drove past the grocery store on her way home, she pulled into the parking lot to shop for tonight's dinner. She only needed a few things, so when she returned to her car, she didn't bother opening the trunk; she piled the items on the floor of the back seat.

That's when she noticed that there was a paper sack already there. Opening it, she saw two very expensive bottles of local Michigan red wine. Earl had no money to buy the wine, so the package had to have been there when he stole the car.

She couldn't drink the wine, but no way was she going to hand the car back to Earl with the wine still in it. A sudden thought made her grin. Steve had to have a birthday; she just didn't know when it was. The two bottles of wine would make a wonderful birthday gift.

With that thought, when she got home she hid the sack in the back of her closet behind a pile of clothes to be given to Goodwill.

Chapter 38

Life for Addie had become an emotional rollercoaster. With the knowledge that Jeb was in serious trouble because of her follow-up letter, her nights were filled with remorse and bad dreams.

But then there was Earl. Her eyes might have dark circles under them, but those eyes were shining. She had found the man of her dreams.

Earl was unique in everything he did. Dinner and a show? With him, the dinner was a simple picnic, and the show was the night sky. Long walks on the beach, card games, and evenings filled with cuddling were the reasons why her eyes were shining. It was just the two of them, and for her that was enough.

Addie was in love.

In her sex-defected power of reasoning, she didn't question why they never drove his car, and she didn't wonder why she never met any of his friends. Any suggestion of mingling with hers for an event was not met with a rejection, but with a colorful description of some other activity that was much better.

Cuddling was great, but what came after cuddling was even better. After a few weeks of reluctantly sending Earl home at the end of an evening, Addie decided she wanted more.

In a short period of time not only had Earl moved in with her, she was happily cooking his meals and doing his laundry. At first, his constantly changing cars puzzled her until he explained that he bought junk cars, fixed them up, and resold them. According to him, that's what he worked on during the day.

In her smitten condition, anything he did was brilliantly wonderful. The stars in her eyes blocked her ability to see any flaws in her beloved Earl, and even though he had yet to utter anything about marriage, she had no doubt that he would.

The only thing that clouded Addie's euphoria was Jeb Linden. If he were guilty of killing his wife, then she had done a good thing by writing the follow-up letter. But if he were innocent, and her gut-feeling said he was, then she had done a terrible thing.

*****

Evelyn Allen Harper

Earl was still in bed when he heard Addie leave for work. He had hours before she returned, and in those hours he had a lot to do. It was time to get rid of his latest hot car, and for that, he couldn't really plan. Some people have perfect pitch, and some people can write books. What he was good at was recognizing an opportunity when it presented itself. He never knew when it would be; he just knew he would take advantage of it when it happened.

A wave of exhaustion swept over him and the urge to burrow back under the covers was strong. Coming up with activities that didn't require money was getting harder and harder. How long could he keep it up? Thank goodness Addie was so easy to please. Every once in a while he caught himself thinking how nice it would be if he really were the kind of man she thought he was. He wouldn't let himself dwell on the fact that eventually she was going to find out that all he was doing was keeping her away from Steve. For some reason, it bothered him. A lot.

Two hours later he was still driving around looking for that special opportunity. It usually didn't take this long to stumble into a situation that made switching cars easy. All he was accomplishing was wasting the gas he had siphoned from a car in the parking garage yesterday. Not having money sucked. Ellen was getting stingy with bank-rolling the Addie project. Now that she was pregnant, she was sure that honorable Steve would stick with her. Removing Addie from the picture wasn't so crucial anymore.

Ah! There it was, an old green junker with the engine running and no driver in sight.

Earl grinned as he drove away. Now he could go home and crawl back into bed. He wanted to be nice and rested when Addie came home from work. She seemed to like it when he entertained her with stories while she was cooking dinner.

Chapter 39

It had taken her time, tears, and threats to sabotage the Dr. Ask-Me-Anything project to put Addie at a table talking to a shackled Jeb Linden.

Her boss's first reaction to her request was one of disbelief. "You want to do what?" he'd barked.

"Hire a private detective. The police latched onto Jeb because it was the easiest thing to do, and then they stopped looking."

"And you think he's innocent?"

"I'd like to think so, but no one else does."

"You've never even met the man!"

"But I'm still the one who got him into trouble! It's because of my follow-up letter that Jeb is being railroaded. I promise, if a private investigator doesn't find something, I'll shut up. I can't sleep, I've lost weight, I can't write, I can't—"

"All right!" he threw up his hands in resignation. "The magazine will hire an investigator."

Addie gave him a sunny smile. "Now, I have another request."

Mr. Lawson frowned. "You're pushing it, Addie."

"It's just a small one."

He sighed, knowing he couldn't refuse her anything.

"I want to visit Jeb in jail."

*****

Addie studied the slouched body of the man across the table. Looking as if he'd withdrawn from life itself, his dead eyes were searching her face.

"Who are you, and why are you here?" he finally asked.

She swallowed hard. Michigan didn't have the death penalty, so because of her, this man would probably spend the rest of his life in prison.

"First let me say that you and I both live on the peninsula, so we're almost neighbors. And I can also say that I noticed a new evening jogger who had to be Cindy. I'm very sorry for your loss, and I'm even sorrier that you're being accused of murdering her."

Jeb looked at her, his eyes puzzled. "They let you in here to console me? Are you a social worker?"

Addie lowered her eyes. "I'm Dr. Ask-Me-Anything."

His head jerked up. "You! You're the one who sent that damn follow-up letter!"

"What can I say? I was truly concerned over your situation and wondered if my advice had helped."

"Help? Lady, you signed my death warrant!"

She hung her head. "Believe me, I feel awful."

"Well, you should. Tell me, was I the only lucky one or do you follow up on all the requests that come in?"

She shook her head. "Only yours. Yours was the only envelope that had a return address on it."

Jeb covered his face with his hands. Wherever Cindy was, he hoped she was listening to this conversation, knowing that he'd be jailed for the rest of his life because of her damn obsessive attention to detail.

"If you came to apologize, I say screw you, lady. Now I want to go back to my cell."

"No, no! That's not the only reason I'm here. Jeb, I don't think you're getting a fair break. Since the police are too lazy to look any further than you, my boss has hired a private investigator."

His eyes flew open. "You believe me when I say I didn't kill my wife?"

"I say you're innocent until they prove that you're guilty. I'm counting on the investigator finding something that will cause enough reasonable doubt to get you out of here."

Tears filled Jeb's eyes. "Listen, believe me, I loved my wife. There's no history of anything being wrong with our marriage, but since we didn't socialize with the neighbors or with other couples, there's no one to vouch for our relationship."

"I'm so sorry, Jeb. If there is anyone out there who can help, the investigators will find them."

Jeb crossed his fingers.

"How are they treating you in here?"

He shrugged. "I get fed, I get to exercise in the yard a couple of times a week, and I'm allowed to shower every third day. But no one will tell me anything. Where is my wife's body? Will there be a funeral? Who will pay for the funeral? I sure can't. What about my house payment? Has the electricity and heat been turned off? Oh, I forgot about my car! It was being worked on and the mechanic was supposed to deliver it to my house. And who assigned that idiot lawyer to defend me?"

If there wasn't an advocate assigned to cases like this, there should be.

"Listen, Jeb. I'll look into hiring someone to take care of your concerns. In the meantime, I just wanted you to know that I'm in your corner working to get you out of here."

Tears were running down his cheeks. "I'd like to thank you, but I don't know your name."

"I'm Addie, Adeline Parker."

"Well, just knowing that you are trying to help me means so much. So, thank you, sweet Adeline."

"I'll stay in touch, Jeb."

*****

Earl was dead broke. Ellen was reveling in her pregnant state now that Steve had accepted the responsibility of fatherhood. With the urgency gone to keep Addie out of the picture, instead of handing him money, she nagged him to get a job.

And then there was Addie who'd been moping around for weeks. In the middle of this, her first reaction to his new green junker car was, "Oh, my boss has a car just like that! It even has the same smashed left fender."

That set him into a panic and back to the streets looking for a replacement.

But today Addie was different. Her face glowed, her eyes weren't tired-looking, and she was smiling.

Earl greeted her. "Well, would you look at my girl this morning! Something sure is making her happy!"

"Oh, Earl, I'm so relieved! I never told you what's been bothering me because it's a work problem. But things are looking so much better!"

"Honey, why didn't you talk to me? You know I'm a good listener."

"Yes, you are! But I hated to admit to you that I caused the problem to begin with. I guess I was embarrassed."

He stepped behind her, put his arms around her and pulled her close. "What kind of a relationship do we have if we can't support each other?" Burying his nose in her hair, he kissed the back of her neck. "Now tell me what's going on?"

Addie bit her tongue. Earl had no idea that she was Dr. Ask-Me-Anything. Why hadn't she kept her mouth shut?

"Have you been following the news story about the guy who's in jail, accused of murdering his wife?"

"The jogger?" he asked.

Addie nodded.

Earl was glad he was standing behind her and she couldn't see his face. "What about it?"

"Word is that a private investigator has dug up some evidence that could shatter the case the cops have against the husband."

His arms tightened. "What kind of evidence?"

"Hey," she complained. "Easy on the hug. I can't breathe."

"Sorry."

"Well, they never did find the murder weapon, but a neighborhood kid has been accusing everyone he runs into of stealing his lucky bat. He said that he'd left on his front yard. Turns out a bat could be the weapon that killed her."

Earl's heart lurched; he'd buried the bat. "How does that help the husband? Couldn't he have picked up the bat?"

Addie shook her head, "They found two neighbors who described a woman on a bicycle who'd made several passes around the jogger, slowing down each time to look at her. They both say they could recognize the rider again."

Earl was having trouble breathing. "Wait a minute. Just because the woman rode around the jogger the cops think she murdered her?"

"Why not? The cops threw Jeb in jail because he had a lousy alibi. Well, there are other things that don't make him look completely innocent, but now that another person could be involved, that should take the pressure off Jeb."

"And why does that make you happy? Do you even know this Jeb?"

"Uh, know him? Not really."

"Come on, Addie. You've groused around here for days over a man you don't even know?"

She knew she was boxed in, so she just shook her head. "I can't say any more because it's a work thing."

Sweet Adeline

Earl moved his arms from around her waist and let his hands sweep up to her shoulders, massaging as he moved toward her neck.

This could complicate things.

Chapter 40

An impatient Addie kept one eye on her computer and one eye on Mr. Lawson's office. It was almost noon and he had yet to make an appearance. Because it was such an unusual occurrence, it was causing a sense of uneasiness to bubble up inside her. He'd left work early yesterday, too, which surprised her because he knew she'd be working late to finish the Dr. Ask-Me-Anything feature for the next issue of *Your World*. Usually she was annoyed when he hung around while she was working, but yesterday she missed him. Plus, he had to approve her finished article before the noon deadline.

It was almost lunchtime when a frenzied Mr. Lawson rushed into his office and slammed the door.

With the deadline hour approaching, she didn't have a choice. His entrance had been so dramatic she was sure he was upset about something. Holding her breath, she tapped on his door.

"What?"

"It's Addie."

"Not now."

"Mr. Lawson?"

"Go away."

"But the deadline—"

There was a slight pause, a sigh, and then in an exasperated voice he called, "I guess you can come in."

Addie opened the door and stopped, alarmed by the sight of her boss's bloodshot eyes. "Mr. Lawson, what happened?"

"Come in and close the door."

"Mr. Lawson—"

There was pain in his eyes when he asked, "It's never going to be Jim, is it Addie? Somehow you just can't bring yourself to call me anything but Mr. Lawson." He sighed. "Right now I need you to call me Jim."

"What's going on, J…J…Jim?"

There was almost a smile on his face. "Now was that so hard?"

Sweet Adeline

"Come on now. You're obviously upset about something and it's not going to be fixed by my calling you Jim."

"You're right. Addie. I didn't sleep last night because I was in jail."

Her mouth fell open. "You? What on earth did you do?"

"According to the police, I stole a car."

"A car? Why would you do that?"

"I didn't say anything about it, but my car was stolen two days ago. I was backing out of my parking space when I remembered that I'd dropped my briefcase when I answered my cell as I was heading for my car. I could see it right there by the front door, so I jumped out of my car to go get it. A car thief drove it off in those few seconds. I reported my car stolen, and then I called a cab and came to work"

"How awful! I can't imagine how you felt when you watched your car being driven away!"

"It sure isn't a good feeling! I was also surprised that a thief would want my old green junker."

What is it with green cars? "So why were you in jail?"

"Well, the next morning I was waiting for the cab to take me to work when I noticed that my car was back and parked in my space!"

"No!"

"Yes! And the keys were in the ignition! So, I waved away the cab, got into my car, and came to work. Yesterday afternoon I left work for an appointment, and on my way back here a police car with his siren blowing pulled me over. Seems I was driving a car that had been reported stolen."

"No!" Addie breathed.

"Yes!" Jim snorted. "No amount of explaining helped, so I was handcuffed, put into the patrol car, and taken to jail where I spent the night."

"No," she whispered.

"Yes! The thief had emptied my glove compartment where I kept the title and insurance information. It took time for me to prove that the car was mine. And then they got angry that I'd probably messed up any fingerprints that the thief had left behind. But whoever stole it hadn't left any prints."

"So you are cleared of all charges?" she asked.

"Yes. I was the one pressing them in the first place so I won't have a police record. The cops were scratching their heads about why the car was returned, but I'd make a bet that some teenager just took it for a joy ride." He sighed. "Well, let's hope that's the last of the green car saga."

"Mr. Law….Jim, I hope so, too! You should go home and get some rest; you really look tired."

"Can't do that! I have a magazine to put to bed, so let's talk about your column."

"I still think most of the letters coming in have been written by frat boys because they are just too funny."

He allowed himself a grin. "I really don't care who writes the letters. The readers are just waiting to read how you belittle and make fun of them with your cutting replies."

Handing him her copy, she turned to leave. "If you approve of what I've written, would you please send it over to Printing? And Jimmy, I'm glad you're out of jail."

Jimmy. That was even better than Jim. He was smiling when she closed the door behind her.

Chapter 41

Steve crumpled the credit card statement in disgust. What the hell was Ellen up to now? Two five-course dinners, enough flowers to fill a room, and according to the statement, she'd been using the charge card to buy groceries. Every week he handed her more than enough cash to put food on their table, so what was she doing with it? Since she was no longer working, he was the only one bringing home a paycheck. Things were going to get a little tight if she kept up this unexplained spending. It was time for a "come to Jesus" meeting, and he wasn't looking forward to it.

She had hinted at being pregnant, but it still hadn't prepared him for the big announcement that she actually was. Before the doctor's appointment, he had felt that even though there were four walls closing in on him, there was an unlocked door that he could escape through. The positive report locked the door.

Some days the trapped feeling left him sweating. There was no way out of his sealed room; Ellen was carrying his child. He had given up following Addie because the good-looking guy was always with her.

Life sucked.

******

Ellen was in the grocery store when her cell phone rang. "Hello?"

"Where the hell are you? You were supposed to meet me an hour ago!"

"Oh, hello Earl."

"Hello yourself! So where are you?"

"Buying groceries."

"But you were supposed to meet me. I need money."

"You always need money, so what's new?"

"Are you forgetting our agreement? I keep Addie away from Steve and you give me money."

"I have Steve so under my thumb right now that he doesn't have time to think of Addie. I know he's not following her anymore."

"So you think you don't need me now? Well, listen up! If you want your little paradise to remain a paradise, you better think twice about cutting me off!"

Silence. And then she asked quietly, "Is that a threat?"

"Could be."

"Earl, I'm not working anymore," she whined. "We made that arrangement when I had money of my own."

"You listen here! You better be paying with your credit card because the cash he gives you for groceries is mine!"

"Uh, Earl? About the grocery money—"

"What about it?"

"I won't have any left over to give you anymore."

"What do you mean 'anymore'?"

"Just what it says. Not anymore. Steve took away my card."

"What?"

"It's your fault, Earl. Those five-course dinners and that shit load of flowers did it. I couldn't explain it so Steve cut up my card."

"What? You can't do this to me!" he yelled.

She held the phone away from her ear.

"No need to yell, Earl."

"We're partners, remember?"

Ellen sighed. "We're partners when it suits you. Right now my hands are tied. I have no money to give you."

"Just like that? You cut me off just like that? What am I supposed to do?"

"Get a job!" she yelled and shut off her phone.

He didn't realize he was gripping his phone so hard until his knuckles were white and his hand complained. The little bitch! There was no way he was going to let her get away with treating him like this while she lived the worry-free good life with Steve. It wasn't fair. Damn! He'd forgotten to tell her that there were two witnesses who could identify her as the woman on the bicycle who'd shown interest in the soon-to-be murder victim.

Grinning, he hit the speed dial button by her name. She needed to have her safe little rosy world messed with; this little bit of news should do it.

Chapter 42

The months went by and the web was tightening around Jeb.

He knew that the lady from *Your World* was frustrated that the information provided by the investigator was being ignored. She had been so sure that the bicycle rider would give the police another suspect besides him, but they weren't interested in finding out who she was.

With no friends and a useless lawyer, Jeb languished in jail watching his life spiraling out of control. Cindy was gone, and so was the wonderful life they'd had together. They had labeled themselves a complete union, one that didn't need to include anyone else. Now he'd give anything to have someone who could vouch for his claim that all had been well with their marriage. His good-for-nothing lawyer was urging him to confess. His promise of a more lenient sentencing if the case didn't have to go to trial hadn't tempted Jeb. Even though the lawyer stated that his punishment would be more severe if they went to trial and he were found guilty, he didn't change his mind. How could he confess to murdering someone he loved when he hadn't done it? Without the possibility of the death penalty, he knew that he would spend the rest of his life behind bars for a crime that he hadn't committed.

The absolute terror of his situation had reduced the robust, happy, loving man into a mere caricature of his former husky self.

Chapter 43

"…and then I thought we could spend a couple of days on Mackinac Island. I know staying at the Grand Hotel is very pricy, but I've wanted to do that for years! My eighth-grade class went there on a field trip, and I'll never forget sitting on the largest porch in the world. Oh, you can't believe the view of the Straits of Mackinac from that porch! And from there we could go—"

Earl tuned out the sound of Addie's voice. For days she'd been planning their next summer vacation. Next summer? Chances were he wouldn't be around next summer, but he played along with her. She was all excited about showing him the wonders of Michigan and if he were still around, he'd like to see what the state had to offer. But he had a problem; he didn't have two dimes to rub together.

He knew he had options; he could just walk away because the deal with Ellen had fizzled out. Steve no longer stalked Addie, and according to Ellen, he was excited about becoming a father. Poor cuckolded bastard!

"…and then, of course, we'd have to come home. Does it all sound good to you?"

Earl nodded his head even though he had no idea what he'd just had agreed to do. But one thing was clear. He needed money.

*****

Several weeks later, Earl entered the kitchen and pecked Addie on the cheek. She was reading the morning paper, completely engrossed.

"Morning," he smiled at her. With a wallet full of money, life was once again sweet.

Addie dropped the paper and looked up. "Do you know how to use a gun?

Earl's body jerked. "Could you wait until I've had my first cup of coffee before you ask me a question like that?" he managed to joke.

"Oh, I'm sorry, love! It's just that reading about the one-man crime wave makes me realize how unprotected we are."

"Did he strike again?"

Sweet Adeline

"Yes. Some poor man had just gotten money from the ATM machine. Just like in those other robberies, the victim didn't get robbed until he was some distance away from the camera."

"Hmmm. I could say he was smart, but doesn't everyone know about the cameras?" Earl remarked as he reached for a bagel. "Any cream cheese in the refrigerator?"

"Should be some on the left top shelf."

"Thanks." Earl opened the refrigerator, and with his back toward her, he waited until his heart settled down. His reaction to her talking about his very own crimes puzzled him. Why did he care? He was eventually going to walk away from her, so why did he want so desperately for her to see him as a good man? In all his years of defrauding women, he'd never had this feeling before.

When he turned around, he had himself under control. "To answer your question, no, I don't know how to use a gun and I have no desire to learn."

Addie gave him a sweet, tender smile before she made the sound of a chicken. "Guess it's up to me then."

"You wouldn't!"

"And why wouldn't I?"

Chuckling, he answered, "You'll shoot your eye out!"

Reaching up, she pulled his head down and kissed him. "Earl, I love it when you make me laugh!"

Chapter 44

The local newspaper was full of news about the comings and goings of the unknown two-bit character actors who were flying into town to attend the trial of their buddy. The presence of the almost famous was much more exciting than the trial of a plain old domestic murderer. If the editor needed copy to fill space, every once in a while a couple of lines might appear on page five.

Jeb was a forgotten man.

He had given up hope; nothing short of a miracle was going to change the outcome and right now he didn't believe in miracles. The one thing he regretted was that the state of Michigan didn't have the death penalty because without Cindy, the world held nothing that interested him; death was much better than life behind bars. He thought of starving himself, but when he mentioned it to his lawyer, he'd scoffed at the idea. "They'd just hook you up and feed you through your veins."

He knew that the lady from *Your World* visited him only because she felt guilty about sending him the follow-up letter. Other than that, he might as well have been in solitary confinement.

He'd lost track of time, so it was a surprise when he heard his lunch coming. The guard usually didn't say anything, but today he actually engaged Jeb in a conversation.

"Hey, looks like you have a pretty good lunch today!" he called out as he approached Jeb's cell.

"What's good about it?" Jeb asked.

"A yummy looking piece of pecan pie! Wonder where that came from?"

"Where does dessert usually come from?"

"The bakery across the street," the guard answered. "They must have put something new on the menu."

Jeb accepted the tray. "What's the weather been like?"

"Well, today it's raining. Really hard, I might add. We've gotten two inches in the past hour. The gutters are overflowing already."

Jeb wished he could come up with something that would make the guard stay and talk to him. But with a rusty brain and a

Sweet Adeline

tongue not used to talking, the guard had walked away before he could think of anything.

Jeb ate his lunch in silence.

*****

Somehow Mary the Baglady had slipped through a crack in the network of social services that had been created for those such as she. Considered the town's character, she lived in a shack near the city dump and survived on handouts from the good citizens and soup kitchens. No one knew her story; she just showed up one day pushing her cart and talking to herself.

While walking through town yesterday she'd noticed a house where an estate sale was going on. From living close to the dump she knew that when the sale was over, many wonderful unsold treasures would end up there. She intended to be the first one to sort through the discarded items.

She hadn't counted on the rain.

The dump was a sea of mud, making it hard to push her shopping cart. The rain was coming in sheets, causing dirt to run in rivulets down her cheeks that hadn't seen water in a long time. Her shack was on the other side of the dump, so in desperation for a shelter of any kind, she headed for the one lone tree that stuck out in the middle of the rusted throwaways.

Spotting it, she abandoned her cart and ran. Reaching the tree, she was thrown to the ground when her right foot stepped into a shallow hole. While thrashing around in the mud trying to get back on her feet, her hand came in contact with something. Out of the mud she pulled a jacket that even covered with black mud she could see it was quite colorful and well made. A treasure was what she'd come to the dump to find, and a treasure is what she found.

Ignoring the rain, she held up the jacket and let the rain wash off the mud. Clutching her prize, she found an abandoned car to shelter her until the rain stopped.

The rain didn't last forever, so when the sun had dried it, Mary left the dump wearing a colorful jacket with the name Cindy Linden sewn into the lining.

"Silly lady, throwing away her pretty jacket, so silly," Mary mumbled to herself as she pushed her cart into town.

Chapter 45

Ellen waited until Steve went back to the morning paper before she trusted herself to pour coffee into his cup. Earl's initial phone call had knocked her peaceful world into a tailspin. His second call just now was just to remind her how delicate her situation was. "Just one little word in the right ear Ellen, that's it."

She shivered. Oh, to be able to go back and undo the stupid decisions to steal the jacket off a jogger. She hadn't needed a jacket, and if she had, she had the money to pay for it. The whole thing had been a throwback to her former life when she had done stupid things without a second thought. Earl had been there to get her out of more messes than she wanted to think about. Because of him, she didn't have a police record but there wasn't anything he could do about this one.

Thinking of him, she realized they hadn't had a real conversation about money since she'd told him that he couldn't count on handouts anymore. It was not like him to accept rejection without some sort of reprisal.

A wave of fear swept through her. What if the payback was something so terrible that he needed time to lay the groundwork? Not only had she watched him do this in the past, she'd often helped him set the stage to bring someone down.

Knowing what he was capable of was making her heart pound. What did he have on her that he could threaten to reveal to the authorities if she didn't give him what he wanted? The answer staggered her. He was the only one who knew where the jacket and bat were.

No, no! Was he going to ruin the life she had with Steve? True, Steve hadn't touched her since she told him she'd quit taking the pill, but at least he wasn't following Addie. He'd helped her set up the nursery, went with her to pick out the paint, and agreed to attend birthing classes with her. Her one reoccurring problem was making up believable excuses to keep him away from her check-ups with the doctor. Life wasn't perfect, but it was better than anything else she'd ever had.

Sweet Adeline

When Steve lowered the paper and smiled at her, the pure joy of being his wife swept away the bad thoughts. And then out of the blue she remembered seeing the City Hall record of her previous marriage. She'd told Earl there wasn't one, but what would stop him from looking it up himself? Was that how he was going to crush her happy home?

Dropping the piece of toast she was holding, she jumped out of her chair and headed for the bathroom.

When noise of her losing her breakfast reached the kitchen, Steve looked up from his paper and frowned. Hadn't Ellen passed the nausea stage a while ago?

He looked back at the paper and realized he'd lost interest in reading it. Even in the best of time with Ellen, reality had a way of slamming him hard; he didn't love her.

But Ellen's pregnancy announcement had shot down the divorce option. He still didn't like her and everything she did irritated him, but there was something to be said about watching a woman growing your child inside her body. What he felt now was a combination of doom and an acceptance of his situation, and perhaps just a little bit of excitement at the prospect of being a father.

Chapter 46

Addie reached out her one free arm and silenced the alarm clock, trying not to disturb Earl who was curled up beside her. His beautiful face, serene in sleep, was just inches from hers. How lucky she was that this amazing man had chosen her. A strong feeling of contentment swept over her; this felt so right.

Falling in love with Earl had been the most exciting thing she had ever done. How could she not love him? He was fun, he was easy to live with, he made her laugh, and best of all, he loved her. Could marriage and a house in the country filled with kids, dogs and love be far behind? The urge to reach out and touch his beautiful face was strong, but knowing what that would lead to, she didn't do it. She needed to get to work.

How did it get to be so late? She pushed Earl's arm off her shoulder, untangled the sheet, and swung her feet to the floor. Thirty minutes. She had to be out the door in thirty minutes or she'd be late again.

A quick shower, a few minutes with the hair dryer, a dab of makeup; she was making good time. At this rate she'd be ready ahead of schedule. Once fully dressed, she was in the process of putting on green dangling earrings that matched her outfit when one skidded off the dresser and fell to the floor.

The earring had disappeared. Crawling around on her hands and knees she enlarged the search area to include the corner of the room that Earl had taken over. She'd been amazed at how few things he'd brought with him when he moved in.

Ah! There it was, right behind his briefcase. In her rush to grab it, the bumped case fell over, sending a couple of papers sliding across the floor. Searching for the lost earring had used up all that was left of the thirty minutes and now she had to waste more time putting things back.

It wasn't that she was trying to read what was on the papers she was retrieving, but when she was shoving two of them back into the case, her hand froze.

Shock, curiosity, and confusion battled for dominance. Her horrified eyes didn't want to believe what her shaking hands were holding. She closed her eyes, hoping that when she opened them the title and the certificate of insurance for James Allen Lawson's car would disappear.

They didn't.

Stunned, she just sat there holding the two damning pieces of paper. Even though she wanted Earl to have a good explanation of how these things had ended up in his briefcase, in her heart she knew that he couldn't have one. She'd seen him driving the green car identical to Mr. Lawson's and with her own ears she'd heard her boss say that he'd spent the night in jail because the thief had taken all his identification out of the glove box.

The thief, he'd said. Earl was the thief.

She jumped when she noticed that he was awake and sitting up. "Hey Babe! You still here? Aren't you going to be late for work?"

Thankful that her back was keeping Earl from seeing what she was doing, she hurriedly crammed the two papers back into the case. That's when her hand touched something big, hard, and cold; it was a gun.

She could hear the covers rustling as he got out of bed. "Hey Luv, why are you crawling around on the floor?"

Thinking fast, she waved the earring and stammered, "I…I…lost an earring, but see? I just found it! Now, I've really got to rush! Go back to sleep, Earl."

She ran out of the room as if the Devil himself were chasing her.

*****

He waited until the sound of the front door slammed shut before he rushed to his briefcase. He'd been awake for the whole earring episode so he was aware that she was looking for it in the area where he had dumped his things.

What had she seen? Had she done more than just pick up an earring?

The briefcase was right where he'd put it. With a sigh of relief, he was about to crawl back into bed when the urge to look inside the case hit him. Knowing he wouldn't be able to sleep until he checked, he went back to the case and opened it.

That's when he saw Lawson's crumpled documents.

*****

Evelyn Allen Harper

Her whole body was shaking, making it impossible for her to insert the key into the ignition. How long had he been watching her? Even if he didn't know that she was on to him, she could never go back and pretend things hadn't changed. What else was he doing in addition to stealing cars? He always had money, so where was he getting it? Remembering their conversation about the one-man crime spree that was happening in her little town, she gasped. That's when she'd asked him if he knew how to use a gun. Oh, shit! Was she in danger? What if he were coming after her right now to silence her? She needed to get out of here.

Earl's newest car that sported different license plates, a pasted-on decal and a bike rack, was parked right beside hers. It was another one of his junkers that he claimed he was going to fix up and sell. Now she knew it was just another stolen car.

When the key finally slipped into the ignition, she put the car into gear, wishing she had someone to talk to or at least someplace to drive to. But she didn't. Work would be the first place he'd look for her.

Her wonderful life had been blown to smithereens by the search for an inexpensive earring she'd bought at the drugstore.

Chapter 47

"You can't do this to me!" Ellen whispered into her cell phone. Leaving Steve and her warm bed, she rushed to the bathroom and closed the door.

"You can, and you will, Ellen. I'm in trouble."

"Albert, how could you have been so stupid? Why in hell did you keep those things?"

"It's Earl, not Albert, and you better not forget that. Can you believe that out of all the cars out there waiting to be stolen, I picked her boss's car?"

"You didn't!"

"I did. I panicked when Addie saw my new fixer-upper and announced that her boss had a car just like it. Of course I ditched it right away, but in the rush, I just forgot to get rid of the documents. But what's done is done, and now I need you to come and get me."

"Why? Knowing you, there's a freshly stolen car just waiting to take you anywhere you want to go."

"Are you crazy? If Addie is doing what I think she's doing, the cops will be looking for the latest car that's been reported stolen."

Ellen was quiet for a moment. She'd been sick with worry that Earl was going to use their secret marriage as a blackmail tool. If she helped him hide, then she's have a bargaining card to hold over his head. "And where would I be taking you?"

"I'd like to be able to go back to your old house, but I can't."

"And why is that?"

"I've taken Addie there several times. She's sure to tell them about it."

"My house? Oh, you bastard!" she wailed. "Now you've involved me!"

"Not really. You can just say that you had no idea who you'd rented the house to. Now I hope you're getting dressed because I expect you to come and get me in the next fifteen minutes or else."

"Or else what, Earl? Are you threatening me?"

"Of course I'm threatening you! I would imagine the husband who's being accused of murdering his wife would love to get out of jail. Remember, I'm the only one who can tell them where the murder weapon is."

"Nice try, asshole! That's not a threat and you know it."

"What makes you think I wouldn't do it?"

"Because you buried it! I just can't see you volunteering information that would get you prison time."

"Don't be so sure. I'm already a repeat offender so if they catch me, I'm going back to jail no matter what. Since I don't have a relationship to wreck and you do, I think you'd better do what I'm asking."

"What am I going to tell Steve? How can I walk out of the house at eight-thirty in the morning and not have him ask me a million questions?"

"He's still there? I expected Steve to be gone by this time."

"He took the day off to go crib shopping with me."

"Little Mother, just think how much you have to lose. I'll see you in what? Twenty minutes?"

Chapter 48

Addie slammed on the brakes, barely missing the bumper of the car in front of her. Her wonderful, considerate, funny, and loving Earl was a thief and a liar. Could she rule out armed robbery and murder?

The memory of making love to him last night brought on another onslaught of tears. It was hard for her to fully grasp the reality of what had happened. She'd woken up this morning in the arms of the man that she loved, and then in the blink of an eye, her whole world had collapsed. That same man was probably driving around right now looking for her…to do what? Would he really hurt her?

The sudden urge to call Steve was so strong she almost ran off the road. For two years, along with being lovers, they had been best friends. When something happened, either good or bad, Steve was the first person to hear about it. She would have been more devastated when she lost him if he hadn't broken up with her in the manner that he had. Showing up already married to Ellen was so bizarre it effectively smothered her feelings towards him. Word was that he'd finally accepted the role of husband and father-to-be, but she still missed him as a friend. No, calling Steve was out of the question.

The jarring blast of a horn startled her. One look at the driver's angry face glaring at her reminded her that driving in such an emotional state was dangerous; she needed to get off the road.

The buzzing of her cell phone startled her. Earl? After all, maybe he hadn't seen a thing this morning. To him, life wouldn't have had a dramatic change. How could she possibly have a conversation with him now that she knew he was a thief and a liar?

She waited until she could pull off the road before she answered it.

"Addie, where are you?"

"Mr. Lawson?"

"You're an hour late for work and yet you sound surprised that I'm calling. What's going on?"

She swallowed hard. Dare she get her boss involved in her problem? She had to tell him something, but what?

"Addie?" he barked. "Are you there?"

She thought all her tears had been used up, but she was wrong.

His voice was much softer when he asked, "What's going on?"

"Mr. Lawson?"

He winced. Was she ever going to see him as anyone other than her boss? "Yeah?"

"Could you meet me somewhere?"

"You mean other than work, where you're supposed to be right now?"

Looking down the road and seeing a small restaurant, she put the car into gear, pulled out into traffic, and drove into the parking lot so that she could see its name.

"Are you familiar with Billy's Bar and Restaurant on 31 going out of town?"

"Very much so."

"Could you meet me there, right now? Please, no questions until you get here." And then she added the magic words. "Please Jim, I need you."

*****

Over coffee and bagels, Addie shared her story with him. It took all the strength he could muster to hide his feeling when she talked about her love for Earl. Finding out who had stolen his car and why it had been returned so quickly was almost humorous.

When Addie finished, he reached over and touched her hand.

"Addie, you do know that you have to notify the authorities."

She blew her nose before she nodded her head. "I know I do, but you can see why I'm scared to do it, don't you?"

"You think he'll come after you?"

"I can't take that chance. If he didn't see anything this morning, he's going to wonder what's going on if I don't show up after work today. But there's no way I'm going back there!"

Jim thought a bit. "You need a place to stay. Right?"

"Yes. A place he'd never think to look."

Sweet Adeline

"Would you consider my apartment to be one of those places?"

Her mouth dropped open.

"No, no, it's not like that," Jim rushed on. "I live with my mother, so you'd be staying with both of us. We have a spare room."

Addie looked across the table at her physically fit and handsome boss who still lived with his mother.

"You look surprised," he grinned.

She just nodded.

"Up until my dad gave me the job of managing *Your World*, I wasn't employed. Mom had to work two jobs just to keep a roof over our heads and food on the table."

"Oh."

"Mom was the only wife out of four to give James Allen Lawson the Second an offspring. It was a short marriage, and I haven't a clue why she left him because she won't ever talk about it except to say that she didn't know she was pregnant when she walked out. Being a single mom, she sometimes ran into trouble trying to support the two of us." Jim rolled his eyes, grimacing. "I've never met my dad, but he did step up financially and put me through college. Gave my mom a bit of a break."

Addie felt the first grin of the day threatening to surface. "So, I'm having coffee with James Allen Lawson the Third?"

He laughed and leaned over the table. "I can see how impressed you are."

"And where is James the Second and why have you never met him?"

"As for where he is, as far as I know he and his fourth wife are living on their yacht somewhere on the Mediterranean. As for why I've never seen him, you'd have to ask him. Wouldn't even recognize him if I ever did."

Other than a sister who lived out of state, Addie had no family. It gave her a warm feeling picturing him and his mother supporting each other.

"So, what do we do now?" she asked.

He grabbed her hand and held on to it. "One of my college roommates is a private investigator. We need to find out who this Earl is. What's his last name?"

"Dixon. Earl Dixon is his name."

She had another cup of coffee while he called Donald Post.

"Thanks, Don. I appreciate it," Jim said hanging up.

"He's working on that name right now. He said he'd get back to me directly, and while we wait, I'll join you in another cup of coffee."

The call came before their cups were empty.

Jim listened, thanked Don, and hung up.

"He says he's just skimmed the surface, but so far there is no record of an Earl Dixon. No Social Security, no nothing."

Addie hung her head. "How could I have been so stupid?"

"Don't beat yourself up. I saw him, Addie. On the outside, he's a good looking guy."

"Beauty is as beauty does," Addie murmured.

Chapter 49

Once outside the police station, Addie scanned the street before she joined Jim on the sidewalk.

"Looking for Earl?" Jim asked quietly.

Addie nodded.

"Scared?"

Addie narrowed her eyes at him.

"Okay, that was a stupid question. Of course you're afraid, but the cops checked and his car is still where you last saw it. You think he saw you going through his case, but maybe he didn't. He could still be in bed for all you know."

"I wish I could believe that!"

"Well, we'll know pretty soon. Sergeant Green promised to call as soon they arrest him."

"So, what now?" Addie asked.

"Now I take you to my apartment and get you settled. Mom won't be there; she's at work."

"Is she still working two jobs?"

"Not since I've been manager of *Your World*. She's working now because she wants to, and not because she has to. I think you'll like my mom. She's a tough cookie!"

Addie smiled and let Jim lead her to his car. She climbed in, wondering if that faint smell of Earl's cologne was coming from her or from the car. Knowing he had sat in this car made her huddle against the door until Jim got in.

"Buckle up," he said putting the car into gear.

*****

"It's the building at the start of the next block," Jim said pointing to the gray and green apartment building.

"Thank you for taking me in," she said softly.

Jim was about to respond when Addie's phone rang making her jump. "It's Sergeant Green," she told him.

Jim watched the expression on her face change; whatever she was hearing wasn't good.

When the call ended, Addie closed her eyes, shuddered and in a despondent voice uttered two words. "He's gone."

Evelyn Allen Harper
*****

"Will you hurry up?" Ellen urged. "Steve's going to wonder why it's taking as long as it is. The story that the replacement at my old job needed more instructions was a good one, but since I might need that excuse again I don't want to wreck it."

Earl gave one last look around. He had run around the apartment with an alcohol-soaked cloth wiping everything he might have touched, while Ellen vacuumed it from top to bottom. Maybe somewhere there was a fingerprint of Albert Linder, but they'd have to work long and hard to find it. The vacuum was probably full of evidence of his presence, so along with Addie's stolen suitcase, he picked them up and headed for the door. He hid from Ellen the overwhelming feeling that he was about to exit the one place in his life that had made him feel content…even happy, because in con games, that's not supposed to happen.

"Where did you park?" he asked.

Ellen shifted an armload of bedding. "Around the corner on the next block. I don't want Steve's car to be involved in any of this."

The sounds of cars stopping and the noise of car doors shutting were all the pair needed to hear.

"The back door," Earl directed.

Chapter 50

If only they'd gotten to the apartment a minute sooner! But they hadn't, and now he had to go back and report to his superior that the man who'd been living with Adeline Parker had skipped. A frustrated Sgt. Green kicked at a piece of cardboard on the sidewalk, and then being a good citizen, he picked it up and tossed it into a trash receptacle.

Things hadn't been going as well as he would like. Missing his man was just the latest one. He was still hung up on his gut feeling that Jeb Linden was innocent, and the more he was around the guy, the stronger he had the feeling. Without a miracle, Jeb was looking at life in prison and it bothered Sgt. Green that Jeb didn't seem to care; he had lost the will to live.

Coming toward him was Mary the Baglady pushing her cart and talking to herself. He called to her. "Good day, Mary! Could I buy you a bowl of soup?"

"Already had one," she answered not looking up from her cart.

He wasn't surprised. The trades' people had accepted Mary, watched out for her, even fed and clothed her.

"That's quite a colorful jacket you're wearing, Mary. Someone give it to you?"

Mary pulled the jacket close and hastened her step. "Didn't steal it!"

Sgt. Green chuckled. She was lucky so many people took care of her, "Have a good day," he called to her and walked on.

He was back at his desk when the memory of the colorful jacket made him pause. Why had it looked familiar?

Chapter 51

Earl pulled his jacket closer and rubbed his cold hands together; he'd never been this cold before.

The cabin Ellen had found was missing every element of gracious living. No electricity, no indoor plumbing, no heat source…not even a fireplace. There was a cooking stove that burned wood, but since he had no matches it was useless. She had left him with some food, mostly canned goods, but no can opener. His cell phone needed charging, too.

Overall, the cabin was a good find because it was evident that it hadn't been used in years, making the chance of being discovered slim. When Ellen came back with all the things he had listed, life would improve.

With nothing to do, he alternated between sleeping on the bare, musty mattress and thinking about his current situation. There was an unfamiliar feeling that was giving him trouble. Hate, lust, greed, revenge, and envy—these feelings he recognized. Come to think about it, what was bothering him was more of an ache than a feeling.

Huddled in a ball, he lay shivering on the bed. If Ellen didn't get here soon, he'd be nothing more than a dead frozen Popsicle.

He slept, and in his dream he could see Addie as she had looked after a night of love. The vision of her tangled red hair and lips swollen from his kisses left him wanting her. It was then that he realized the presence of her in his dream had made the persistent ache inside him disappear. The disgusting truth woke him with a start. Staring at the ceiling of his cold cabin, he faced reality; he was in love with Addie.

Shit.

That wasn't supposed to happen.

Silence had been his partner for so long the pounding on the door was jarring. "I'm coming, I'm coming!" he yelled.

He opened the door and Ellen rushed in. "Don't just stand there, help me unload the car."

Sweet Adeline

"Please tell me you brought some warm clothes! I'm freezing!"

"You'll be worse than freezing if I don't get the car back to Steve in an hour. He's threatening to take the keys away."

"Did you bring everything on the list?"

"The only place that had some of those things was a small theater warehouse. Cheek implants, wigs, mustaches, pot belly cushions …what on earth are you planning?"

"I'm not staying in this Godforsaken freezer any longer than I have to. The next time you come, I'm going back to town with you, so you'd better bring me some money."

"How many times do I have to tell you that I don't have any? Steve is a tight-wad! He has me writing down every penny that I spend."

"Well, I'm not completely broke. I still have some left from my little crime spree."

"That was you? The ATM bandit?"

"Yeah, that and a few other gigs. The trouble with ATMs is that only so much can be taken out at one time."

Ellen laughed. "Poor baby! What's the limit? Five hundred dollars? At that rate, you'd need to bash in a lot of heads just to get spending money."

"Tell me about it!" he chuckled. "Where are the matches and the can opener?"

"I didn't forget them. Now you have enough food to last until I come back in two days. Steve is going out of town with his boss so I'll have the car."

Ellen dropped the rest of the things in her hand and dashed out, slamming the door behind her.

Chapter 52

Addie was thoughtful while driving behind Jim's car on the way to the apartment. The fact that it was her boss's apartment was the problem. Calling him something other than Mr. Lawson was hard enough, and now she was going to be living under the same roof with him.

The only stop was at the drugstore where she bought a few personal items to tide her over until she could send the police into her apartment with a list. No way was she setting foot in there until Earl was captured.

His flashing turn signal alerted her that their destination was on the left. She had driven past these apartments for years and had often wondered what they were like inside.

He and his mother shared a ground floor apartment that had a patio. The apartment was spacious, open and sparsely decorated. When Addie noticed the absence of clutter and commented on it, he laughed and stated that his mom was a believer in minimal decorating. If any new item was brought in, she removed an old one. The master bedroom was situated on one side, with the kitchen and the great room separating it from the other two bedrooms. Since it was an end unit, there was an exit door that opened to the parking garage.

"You and I will be sharing a bathroom. I hope you don't mind."

She sucked in her breath and nodded. The whole situation felt weird. "You're sure your mom won't mind? I feel like such an intruder!"

"I spoke to her about it, and believe me, she's fine. I just know the two of you will get along."

"Look at the time! Don't you have to get back to work?" Addie asked.

"I hate to just drop you off and leave, but I really do have to get back. Come with me and I'll show you my office. There's no reason why you can't do your column from here. Since no one at work knows it's you, I'll just tell them you had to take a leave of absence because of a family problem."

Sweet Adeline

His office was a crowded corner of his bedroom. There was a desktop computer and a printer that was buried under thick stacks of copy paper. Upon closer inspection, Addie could see a title on the top pages with the author's name, James Allen Lawson; they were manuscripts.

"You write?" she asked, her eyes wide.

He was blushing when he said, "You were never meant to see those."

Puzzled, she questioned, "Why are you embarrassed about being a writer?"

"I don't think you can call someone a writer if they've never been published, and believe me, I've never been published."

Addie shook her head. "I've always known I wanted to be a writer. All my college professors praised my work, told me I had 'promise' but have I ever written a book? I haven't even come close to even trying. How many have you written?"

"Four completed ones. It's a series."

"I'm impressed," she said. "*Really* impressed."

He beamed. "I've wanted to talk to you because I recognize good writing when I read it. And you, Addie, are an excellent writer."

It was Addie's turn to blush. "I kept wondering when you were going to let me write something for the magazine that wasn't fluff. You do know that's what you pay me to do."

He laughed. "But you write such excellent fluff! I have to leave now or I'll never get anything done."

Addie thought about the long lonely hours ahead with nothing to do but worry about her situation. "Would you give me permission to read one of your books?"

"Just one of them?" he chuckled. "You have my permission to read all of them, but start with the first one."

Once alone, Addie sat down on Jim's unmade bed and looked around. Clothes were scattered over chairs and on the floor. There were posters still on the wall from his high school days and a shelf full of trophies for football, basketball, softball and track decorated the room. It was completely opposite from the rest of the apartment. Jim seemed to hold on to things. Mr. Lawson might be her boss, but he was also an interesting person who was full of surprises.

Fortunately, the manuscripts were numbered. Finding book one, she immersed herself into the fantasy world created by Mr. Law...Jim.

Chapter 53

He remembered! Joe Green woke with a start and sat up in bed. Baglady Mary was wearing Cindy Linden's jacket! It was a perfect match to Jeb's. He claimed that he and his wife did everything together, so would it be wrong to think they might have matching jackets? His name was on a tag that had been sewn into the lining, and Joe would bet a week's salary that Mary's jacket would have a tag with Cindy's name on it.

Jeb's trial was scheduled to start next month. Word was that Jeb, who had always claimed he hadn't murdered his wife, was now considering confessing just to get the whole thing over with and do away with the trial. His do-nothing lawyer was pushing the idea.

He had to find Mary.

It was a long four hours between four o'clock in the morning and the start of his eight o'clock shift. Sleep was out of the question, so over a cup of coffee he planned what he would do.

He knew Mary spent a lot of her time living in a cabin near the dump. Finding it shouldn't be a problem, but what if she wasn't there? There was no set schedule to her trips into town. He'd seen her at the beginning of his shift, and he'd seen her at the end of his shift. Just the thought of finding a clue that would point the investigation away from Jeb was making him anxious. What if she'd gotten rid of it? So much was riding on his finding Mary and the jacket.

*****

By the time he finally stumbled upon her shack, it was mid-morning and Mary wasn't there. He'd noticed several cars parked at the dump's entrance, probably scavengers looking for discarded unsold items from the estate sale yesterday. With luck, maybe Mary was one of them.

It wasn't a huge dump, and it didn't take him long to spot her digging into a fresh trash deposit. His heart sank when he saw that she wasn't wearing the jacket.

"Mary, where's the jacket you had on the other day?" Joe called to her.

One glance at the sergeant heading toward her was enough to send her running.

"Mary, stop! I just want to ask you a question!" Joe called after her.

Mary just ran faster.

"Please, Mary, stop! I need to talk to you!"

"No, you don't!" she yelled back. "You want to take away my jacket!"

Not only was Joe in better shape than Mary, his legs were a lot longer than hers. It was just a matter of time before he caught up with her.

She was a small woman but a fearless fighter. Joe didn't want to hurt her but she had no qualms about hurting him. He could feel her teeth trying to bite him through his uniform.

"Mary," he tried to sound unthreatening. "Please settle down! I just want to ask you something!"

"It's about the jacket, isn't it? It's my jacket and you can't have it!"

"Mary, what if I told you that your jacket once belonged to a nice lady? She probably had it on when someone killed her."

Mary quit struggling. "She was wearing it when she died?"

Her lucidity was startling.

"Probably."

"I've been wearing the jacket of a murdered woman?"

Joe nodded, "It could help us find the killer."

Mary rubbed her arms and shuddered. "Follow me."

It was a short trip to the lone tree in the dump. Mary stopped and pointed to a spot under it. "I could tell that you thought I'd stolen the jacket, so I hid it back in the hole where I found it."

Without a shovel, Joe knelt at the spot and dug with his hands. It didn't take him long to uncover the jacket along with a bat – the possible murder weapon. Upon inspection, the tag sewn onto the lining was caked with mud, but Cindy's name was still readable.

While Sgt. Green was savoring the joy of finding the jacket and the murder weapon, he knew that it didn't remove Jeb from being a subject. True, it was just a short period of time between finding the victim and his knocking on Jeb's door, but it was enough even if you counted Jeb's short walk. But why would Jeb want to bury his wife's jacket?

*****

150

Sweet Adeline

Jeb sat across the table from Sgt. Green and stared off into space. He knew there was nothing new that the cop could tell him, so why even listen? His eyes drooped, and then closed while his visitor's voice droned on and on.

"...and then, I reached my hand into the hole and pulled out Cindy's jacket."

Jeb's eyes flew open and he sat up. "What?"

"Haven't you been listening?" Sgt. Green barked. "Pay attention, Jeb. I found Cindy's jacket and the murder weapon buried in the dump."

"In the dump?" Jeb's eyebrows shot up. "What were they doing at the dump?"

"Cindy's killer buried them there."

His face lit up. "You found the killer? That means I'm out of here!"

"Not so quick! The authorities are going to say that you are the one who buried the evidence."

"Me? Why would I bury Cindy's jacket? Of course I didn't do it!"

"But you had time, Jeb. It would have been close, because there wasn't much time between when the body was found and the time it took me to get to your house, but I think it can be proven that it was enough for you to do it and be back home when I rang your bell."

Jeb's face fell back into a defeated mask. "So, I'm still going to be charged with her murder."

Sgt. Green nodded. "I tried, Jeb. I really thought I could find something that would exonerate you because I do think you're innocent."

He was halfway to the door when Jeb's excited voice stopped him. "I couldn't have made the trip to the dump, Sgt. Green."

Turning around, Joe didn't see the usual defeated face but one that was bright and filled with hope. "My car was in the garage! Cindy and I had been going back and forth to work in a taxi. As far as I know, the mechanic still has my car!"

*****

It didn't take long to establish that the mechanic really did have Jeb's car because he couldn't find anyone to return it to, and that the one taxi company in town stated that none of their cabs had made a trip to the dump.

It took time, but all charges against Jeb were dropped. When he finally walked out of jail a free man, Sgt. Green personally took him to the best restaurant in town, bought him a steak dinner, and then drove him home to a dark house.

Jeb didn't make a move to get out of the car. Instead, they sat there in silence for some time, the sergeant not saying a word about the tears that were running down Jeb's cheeks; he could only guess what was going through his mind.

Jeb finally wiped his face on his sleeve. The reason why Cindy had taken up jogging would forever remain a mystery. "I guess I have to go in there, but I sure don't want to."

Sgt. Green didn't open his mouth because there was nothing he could say that would give Jeb his life back. His wife was gone but the house he was about to enter would be full of her.

Jeb turned and held out his hand. "Sgt. Green, you saved my life, and I will forever be in your debt."

"I'm sorry this happened to you," Joe said as he shook Jeb's hand.

With that, Jeb got out of the car and walked slowly toward his house.

Sgt. Green waited until Jeb was inside before he drove off. Maybe now the investigators would follow up on other leads.

Chapter 54

Addie was halfway through book one when the rattling of a doorknob alerted her that someone was about to enter the apartment. Since it was too early for either Jim or his mother, Addie looked for a place to hide. Could Earl have found her?

The door swung open to reveal a woman who looked to be in her thirties. Tall and slim, her long black hair was swept to the side with the length of it draped over one shoulder. Impeccable make-up and a coordinated outfit gave the woman an air of sophistication that made Addie absentmindedly smooth down her sweat suit. Who was this woman? Too young to be Jim's mother. Wait a minute. Could she be Jim's girlfriend? Oh, how awkward this was going to be!

Spying Addie peeking around the corner, the woman's face brightened. With a smile, she opened her arms and rushed towards her. "You must be Addie!" she cried. "I am so glad to finally meet you!"

Addie found herself smothered in the arms of a woman who was much taller than she and who smelled heavenly. This was Jim's mother?

"Mrs. Lawson?" her voice muffled.

"No, no! Certainly not Mrs. Lawson, at least not anymore! My name is Beth," she laughed.

It wasn't easy to breathe in her squashed position, but Addie managed to say hello.

After Addie managed to pull herself out of the embrace, she asked, "Uh, aren't you home early? Jim said you would be home around six o'clock."

"I took off early because I'm going to a big party tonight, plus I was just dying to meet you! I'm going to tell you a little secret. You are the first girl Jim has ever brought home. It must be really serious between the two of you for Jim to do something as drastic as letting his girlfriend meet his mother!" She was laughing.

Addie froze. What had Jim told her? Didn't his mother know that she was here only because she was afraid to be anywhere

153

else? How dare he lie to his mother about their relationship! Well, just wait until he comes home!

"What have you done all day? It must have been lonely being here all by yourself."

"Oh, no!" Addie stepped back, putting distance between them in case Beth might decide she needed another hug. "I've been reading the first book in Jim's series."

Beth's eyes widened. "He let you read it?"

"Why, yes! He said I could read his books."

Beth looked pensive. "He won't let me read what he writes."

"Really? He's a good writer! Does he give you a reason why he won't let you read his work?"

She shook her head.

Addie grinned. "Well, if I wrote sex scenes as hot as your son writes them, I wouldn't want any of my relatives to read them, either."

Beth ended up laughing so hard she backed into a chair and plopped down. "Oh my!" she said as she wiped her eyes. "He must think he needs to shield his poor sainted mother from the facts of life."

Addie looked puzzled. "I don't understand."

"He knows my marriage to his dad was a real short one. In fact, it was just a few weeks after we were married that I left. I caught him in bed with the live-in maid." Beth had to wait for Addie's astonished mouth to close before she added, "As far as Jim knows, those few days are the extent of my sex life."

Addie put the live-in-maid information on hold to think about later because right now she was feeling guilty about telling Beth about Jim's books. If Jim hadn't told his mother about them, she shouldn't have either. "Beth, I think I should have kept my mouth shut about Jim's writing. If he wanted you to know what was in them, he would have told you himself. Could I please ask you to pretend that we never had this conversation?"

"Believe me, Addie, you don't have a problem; I won't ever mention it. My son and I might share this apartment, but we rarely see each other. He comes and goes from his part of the unit, and I do the same from my end. Would you believe that we have to make appointments ahead of time if we need to talk?"

So Jim wasn't a mama's boy after all.

Sweet Adeline

She continued. "He told me about you in a phone conversation. It was the day of the big rain that caused a lot of static on the line, but I'm sure I got most of his message."

Addie felt some of the steam leaking out of her plan to pounce on Jim for letting his mother think that she was his girlfriend.

"Well, it was nice meeting you, Addie, but I have dinner plans for tonight and I need to get ready. I'm sure Jim will come up with something for the two of you to eat," she exclaimed as she turned to leave. "Not much cooking goes on around here."

Beth rushed out of the room taking most of the oxygen with her, leaving Addie with her mouth hanging open.

Chapter 55

Expecting to see Earl answering her knock, Ellen jumped back after the door of the shack opened to reveal a threatening-looking scruffy brown-eyed man with no hair filling the entrance.

"Yeah?" he snarled.

"Oh, my God," she cried. "Who are you? And what have you done with Earl?"

"Earl? Was that the name of the sniveling excuse-of-a-man that I buried under a pile of dirt at the back of the shack?" the man growled. Taking a step toward her he threatened, "There's plenty of room for another pile back there, if you know what I'm gettin' at, lady."

Her brain screamed at her legs to run, so while both hands clutched at her belly, that's what she did. She almost made it to her car when she realized the man was laughing.

"Oh, Ellen, it's me! I wish you could see the expression on your face!"

"E...E...Earl?"

"Of course it's me! Oh, that was funny!" After wiping his face with his sleeve, he added, "Just wait until you see me when I put on my pot belly and do away with the dimples with cheek expanders and my...."

Ellen's fist hit his nose.

"What the hell?" he yelled.

"That's what you get for scaring me to death!"

"That hurt!" he grumbled, rubbing it. "Come on in. We have some planning to do."

"I'm still shaking! You shouldn't scare a pregnant woman like that, you jackass!" she complained while patting her stomach. "I need a drink, but I can't have one because of this kid."

"Speaking of the kid, who is the guy you picked up that night at Joe's?"

"Never saw him before that night, and I haven't seen him since, even though I've gone back to Joe's looking for him."

Sweet Adeline

"I'll bet you have! With Steve not touching you, I'm not surprised that you went looking for him. Were you hoping to have another romp in the hay?"

She laughed. "You sure know me, Earl! No, we didn't exchange names. All I remember is that he had a funny hairline in the front. It kinda came down to a point."

"That's called a widow's peak, an inherited thing. Did the guy have dark hair?"

Ellen nodded. "Really dark, almost black. What are you getting at, Earl?"

"Well, as I recall, both you and Steve have blonde hair and blue eyes. I think you'd better start making up stories about your dark-haired relatives, dead of course, because that kid you're carrying could be sporting a black widow's peak."

Ellen flopped down on a chair. "Oh, my God! I never thought what this kid was going to look like. I just needed it to make Steve stay with me. Now what?"

"Like I said, it's not too early to start making up stories about your dead relatives."

Ellen burst into tears. "I just can't stand the thought of losing this thing I have going on with Steve. I'm a happily married woman with a baby on the way, something that I never thought I'd ever be!"

"That's where planning ahead comes in. You do your thing with made-up relatives and chances are you'll come out of this smelling like a rose. Now it's my turn to plan."

"Are you really going back to town with me today?" she asked, wiping the last of the tears off her face.

"That's the plan. You can drop me off at that little bed and breakfast place. I'll stay there until I can find a furnished room to rent."

"You are going to stay in your disguise? And what name are you going to use?"

"Of course I have to stay in disguise! I'm sure every agency in town is looking for me. As for the name, why can't I use my real one? I kinda miss being called Albert."

Ellen shook her head. "That's not a good idea. No reason to help them find you in case you missed a fingerprint or two in Addie's apartment. So, let's pack up your stuff and head for town. Steve's away and I might just have to go out and play tonight."

Earl snickered. "With that belly of yours, do you really think you'll find a partner who thinks screwing a pregnant woman is sexy?"

Ellen hit him again.

Chapter 56

Something evil was getting closer and closer, ripping away her ability to think. She needed to scream, but no sound came out when she tried.

Just as evil was about to pounce, Addie jerked awake.

Where was she? The room was dark and unfamiliar, her heart was pounding, her mouth was dry, and her pajamas were sticking to her sweat-drenched body. She couldn't move. She had to move!

As she untangled the sheet that was holding her prisoner, yesterday's events raced through her mind. Hell. The nightmare was almost as scary as reality. She was in her boss's apartment because she was hiding from Earl who, up until yesterday morning, was the love of her life.

She flipped over in bed, grabbed a pillow and hid under it. How could she have been so trusting, so blind, so dumb? She threw the pillow away wishing that she could do the same with her memories along with her broken heart. Twice in such a short time she had been blindsided by the men she thought she loved and whom she thought loved her back.

She'd been sure that Earl loved her. Hadn't he told her many times that he did? It was hard to believe that none of it had been real. But for what reason? He obviously was a conman, but why had he picked her? She didn't have a lot of money, and she didn't have connections to anything that would benefit him. So why her? The police were adamant about her staying hidden until he was found.

Feeling the sweat drying on her skin was making her uncomfortable. Sharing a bathroom with her boss felt weird, but they had made rules that seemed to be working. Jim had first dibs on the shower because he had to go to work and she didn't. Since it was still early, she figured that she could shower and be back in her room before he woke up. Grabbing her things, she headed for the bathroom.

A few minutes later, she was puzzled when the water turned cold. Grabbing a towel, she was drying her dripping red hair when she heard a quick intake of breath. Whirling around, she saw the back of Jim as he rushed out of the room.

"I'm sorry!" he yelled from the other side of the door he had just slammed shut. "I...I...I didn't see a thing! Honest!"

Startled, she opened her mouth to howl in protest, but quickly closed it. There was no reason for him to think that she'd be in the bathroom this early, plus she hadn't locked the door. What was done was done, but it sure was going to make for an interesting breakfast. Did he really believe she bought his story that he hadn't seen anything?

She quickly wrapped a towel around her, gathered her things and yelled, "It's your turn, but there's no hot water!"

Later, Jim walked in while she was seated at the table nibbling on a piece of toast. Not even glancing her way, he poured himself a cup of coffee and left. She heard the front door close and the sound of his car door opening. Since her car was hidden inside the garage, he had to park on the street.

Was he really going to leave without saying anything? She ran to the window and looked out, hoping that he'd just gone to his car to get something and then he'd come back in so that they could talk about the bathroom incident.

As she watched, he started the car and drove away.

She was still standing there when Beth's voice startled her. "Good morning. Something going on out there? Thanks for making coffee."

"Oh, good morning, Beth," she answered in a distracted manner.

"You don't sound very cheerful this morning. Did the cold water surprise you when you took your shower? There must be something wrong with the water heater. I've called building maintenance."

Addie nodded. "It was a shock, but that's not what's bothering me."

"Are you getting tired of being a prisoner?"

Addie turned away from the window and saw Beth looking at her with concerned eyes. Jim's mother was not only stunningly beautiful; she was one of the nicest people Addie had ever met. When he'd told her that his mother had worked at two jobs to support them, Addie had pictured a mousy little woman who cleaned houses and scrubbed floors. Her two jobs turned out to be

Sweet Adeline

modeling for a rival magazine and managing a modeling agency. In her gray sweat suit Addie felt like a dull pigeon compared to colorful Beth.

Since Beth was usually up and out of the apartment before Addie got up, the two of them had never had a real conversation. Pouring herself another cup of coffee, she took her cup and sat down across the table from Beth.

"I don't mind the solitude because I'm reading Jim's manuscripts and doing my...my magazine work on his computer."

Beth grinned. "I know it's you, so you can say the good doctor's name. Do you know that Jim credits you for saving his magazine?"

"So he says," Addie said quietly.

"What's bothering you, Addie?"

She studied Beth's face before she said, "I'd love to tell someone what's been driving me crazy, but it's a long story. Are you sure you have time?"

Beth leaned back in her chair. "I'm not expected at the office until after lunch."

Addie took a big breath. "My big question is why me? Why did Earl go to such trouble to get involved with me? If I ever have the chance to talk to him again, that's the one question I'd ask him."

"Whoa! I think I need another cup of coffee to fortify me for the story about this Earl guy who I know nothing about," Beth remarked. "I was under the impression that Jim was bringing his girlfriend here because she had to hide for a couple of days. But you aren't his girlfriend, are you?"

"No, I'm not."

"The way my son talks about you, I thought you were."

Addie sighed. "Jim is probably the most decent, honorable man that I've ever known. Unfortunately, I keep getting involved with men who are neither decent nor honorable."

"So it's this Earl guy that you're hiding from? Is he a threat to you?"

"I'm scared enough to have nightmares about him." She shivered and rubbed the bumps on her arms.

"That bad, eh? So, tell me about Earl."

Addie thought for a moment before plunging into a story that would make her relive the life and death of the greatest love of her life.

Taking a deep breath, she started the story.

"It was so easy to fall in love with him…."

Beth's coffee grew cold as she listened.

"…and then somewhere in this time frame, Jim's car was stolen and Earl came home with a new fixer-upper, a green car with a damaged fender. I made an innocent remark that my boss had a car just like it. The next day, Earl had a different car."

Beth chimed in. "I think I know the next part of the story. When Jim had his car back, he didn't report finding it to the police but drove it to work. That's when he went to jail for driving a stolen car."

"That's right. Because whoever had stolen his car had taken everything out of his glove box. Jim told me he went to jail because he couldn't prove the car was his. Beth, I'm having trouble believing that my fairytale life came to an end just a few days ago. How can I go from being deeply in love with Earl to having nightmares about him now? That's what woke me up this morning."

Beth had a faraway look in her eyes. "If anyone can understand, I can. I was deeply in love with my husband up until the live-in-maid incident."

Addie winced. "That must have been awful!"

"He laughed at me for being so upset and claimed the whole thing had been a misunderstanding. He said I didn't have a good sense of humor."

"What did you do then?"

"I hauled off and punched him in the nose. It was still bleeding when I walked out the door. Good thing I didn't know that I was pregnant or I might have stayed because of the baby."

No one spoke. Finally, Beth broke the silence. "Finish the story, Addie."

Addie closed her eyes and pictured that last morning. She and Earl had made love several times during the night and the last thing she wanted to do was leave his warm arms.

"What are you remembering?" Beth whispered.

Addie opened her eyes. "I was reliving the last moments of a fairytale. Because I stayed too long in bed, I had thirty minutes before I had to run out the door. Your son runs a tight ship, Beth. If we aren't sitting at our desks at the stroke of nine, we're late."

Beth chuckled.

Sweet Adeline

"In my rush, I dropped an earring, and ended up on my hands and knees looking for it. Now is the time to make the sound of a drum roll, because here comes the big finish. This is where my life gets blown to smithereens. Ready?"

Beth just nodded.

"Okay. I finally found the earring behind Earl's briefcase, which I proceeded to bump and when it fell over, some papers slipped out. I was in a big hurry because I'd used up my thirty minutes looking for the earring, so I really didn't mean to read the documents, but it was hard to miss the name of James Allen Lawson on a car title and certificate of insurance. And then Earl was sitting up in bed watching me, but since my back was to him, I didn't know what he'd seen. While I was stuffing the papers back in, I found a gun on the bottom of the case. Remember the ATM crime spree? The police are pretty sure it was Earl."

"Oh, how frightening! Did you confront him?"

"All I could think about was getting out of there! I waved the earring and yelled that I'd found it. Beth, I ran for my life."

"What about him? Is he still living in your apartment?"

"No, according to the police, when they checked there was no trace of him left in my apartment. He used something, probably alcohol, to wipe my apartment from top to bottom. The police couldn't find a clear fingerprint, and there were none in the stolen car he left behind. He had to have someone helping him because in the time I left the apartment and the time the police got there, my entire apartment had been vacuumed and completely cleaned. My new vacuum is missing, and he stripped the bed down to the mattress. He even took all his dirty clothes out of the hamper."

"Why would he do that?"

"He doesn't want his identity discovered. So far, the investigators haven't found any trace of him left in my apartment. Beth, I fell in love with a thief and a liar," Addie took a deep breath and stared down at her hands in her lap. "Earl Dixon doesn't even exist."

"Oh, Addie! I'm so sorry! I didn't know any of this. Jim just asked if he could bring a girl home for a few days. Our phone conversation was full of static, and I admit I didn't hear everything he said, but I had it in my head that you were his girlfriend. I can't tell you how disappointed I am that you're not."

"Jim never had a chance. Before Earl, there was a guy named Steve, but that ended when he returned from a high school reunion with a wife. I was devastated. Jim was trying to make me look at him as a person and not just as my boss, but when Earl entered the picture, he was all I could see."

"Now I understand why Jim has been so grumpy, but he usually never lets anything get between him and his next meal. Do you know why he left this morning without eating breakfast?"

Addie lowered her eyes. "Maybe."

Beth's eyebrows rose in question.

"It was my fault! It wasn't my turn in the bathroom but since he wasn't even up yet, I thought I had time to shower. He walked in and caught me."

Beth threw her head back and laughed. "I'll bet that woke him up in a hurry!"

"I wanted to apologize to him this morning over breakfast, but he wouldn't even look at me. He just grabbed a cup of coffee and ran out the door."

Beth studied the beautiful girl across the table. "Addie, have you ever been in love with someone who didn't love you back?"

Addie thought. "When Steve married his old high school sweetheart, that hurt, but according to him, he still loves me."

"Were you in love with him?"

"I thought I was until I experienced the real thing with Earl. It probably was part of Earl's con, but he constantly told me how much he loved me. But no, I never loved someone who didn't claim to love me back."

"Well, then you have missed out on the most exquisite pain in the whole world."

"You're saying that after he saw me naked, he didn't want to talk to me because he's in love with me?"

"I would imagine he dreams about you, and the sight of your body was enough to send him running out the door. He knows he can't have you."

"Oh, my. You think my being here is causing him that pain you mentioned? Should I find somewhere else to stay until Earl is found?"

"No, I'm sure he wants you here. All I ask is that you don't give him any reason to think you have feelings for him if you don't. That would be a cruel thing to do, Addie."

Sweet Adeline

Addie was left with nothing but her thoughts when Beth finally went to work. The deadline for submitting her column for the next issue was two weeks away, so there was no feeling of urgency to even think about it. The third manuscript was waiting for her, but the desire to read it wasn't there. What she wanted was to lie on her bed and allow scenes from the past couple of months stream through her memory.

Could she ever love another man the way she'd loved Earl?

Chapter 57

Horns blaring, brakes squealing, and voices shouting vile suggestions brought Jim back to the real world. Slamming on his brakes, he backed up full speed and missed by inches of being hit by the oncoming traffic. The ONE WAY TRAFFIC sign was right there for any motorist to see if they were paying attention.

He hadn't really planned on skipping breakfast, it just happened. Seeing Addie already at the table looking as if nothing earthshaking had happened was more than he could handle. Laughing about the incident over coffee was not something he was ready to do, so he ran.

He didn't even have to close his eyes to see the image of Addie with nothing but the towel around her head; the picture was burned into his memory. Knowing that Addie had no romantic feelings for him was killing him.

It was too early to go to the office but not too early to go to the gym and pound the shit out of the swinging bag.

*****

Earl walked the streets in his disguise, looking for Addie. He even did the old trick of getting off the elevator on the sixth floor of her building, pretending to be looking for the law office that he knew very well was on the seventh floor. His eyes had scanned the front office workers hoping to catch sight of her, but she wasn't there. How pathetic was it that he had to see her just to ease the persistent ache inside him. It disgusted him to realize that he was no better than her old stalking boyfriend.

If Addie were hiding, then she'd figured out that he was not her knight in shining armor. For reasons he was trying to understand, he regretted that he wasn't the man that she'd thought he was. It wasn't supposed to end like this. After every other con, he'd been able to walk away with never a backward glance.

As he had on most afternoons, at six o'clock he positioned himself on the opposite side of the street from Addie's building. One of these days, she just had to come out the door and he wanted to be there when she did.

Sweet Adeline

He saw the guy who had to be her boss because he'd watched him drive out of the parking lot in the familiar green car. Stealing that car had been the beginning of the end. What if...?

He shook his head. Playing the what if game never changed anything.

It was time to move on to bigger and better things, and he eventually would. He had to, because the closer Ellen got to her delivery date, the stingier she became about giving him anything.

If only he could find Addie. Sure, she'd be afraid of him at first, but if she'd give him a chance to plead his case, he was sure he could talk his way back into her heart. With her love, he'd leave his old ways behind and become the man that she once thought he was. He could do it...no, he *had* to do it.

Where was she?

Chapter 58

Addie reread her finished Dr. Ask-Me-Anything column for the umpteenth time. Her readers were going to love her answer to Bride-to-Be who wanted to know if she should tell her intended groom before or after the wedding that she'd had a sex-change operation. The one about the husband who was upset because his girlfriend had caught him making love to his own wife was a good one, too. Satisfied that she'd caught all the errors, she hit the Send icon. Jim would go over it and then send it back to her with his corrections. There was always something that his eagle eye would catch that she'd missed.

She leaned back on the chair and stretched. Life had gotten into a routine that had become quite comfortable. Beth and Jim left in the morning before she was awake. Since Beth was on the other side of the apartment, Addie rarely saw her come and go. She did hear Jim in the morning when he took his shower. Ever since the bathroom incident that they'd never discussed, he always tapped on the door before he opened it. Days would pass when she didn't see him at all. In fact, she noticed that his bed hadn't been slept in last night.

Her work done, she walked out of Jim's room and headed for the shower. She'd heard his startled yelp this morning so she knew there still was a problem with the hot water supply.

Suddenly, she remembered. It was during the time early in their affair when she was still sending Earl home at night that a problem had developed in the water heater that maintenance either couldn't or wouldn't fix. He had stepped in and fixed it with a wink and a question: "Wouldn't it be nice to have a handyman like me around all the time?"

Directly after that, she'd asked him to move in with her.

Addie raced to the phone and called Sgt. Green.

"I remembered something!" she yelled when she heard him pick up.

There was a pause before the officer asked, "Addie?"

"Yes, yes, it's Addie!"

"Are you alright?"

Sweet Adeline

"Yes, I just remembered. In my apartment we had a plumbing problem that Earl fixed. Check the water pipes in the basement. I'll bet he never thought of those fingerprints!"

"I'll go check it myself. Thanks, Addie. I'll get back to you if we find anything."

The rest of the day she stuck to the routine of cleaning and planning dinner, not knowing if anyone would be around to eat it. Beth had a life of her own that she didn't share with anyone and Jim had found something to occupy his evenings. It was late in the day when her cell rang.

"Addie, it's Sgt. Green."

Addie held her breath, waiting.

"You were right. We found his prints all over the pipes in the basement. Because of you, we now know who Earl really is."

"Thank God," she breathed.

"His name is Albert Richard Linder. He's a thief with a long record of robberies, breaking and entering, car theft, you name it. He and an accomplice ran a couple of scams, but we have no record of who that accomplice was. He's the one who does the jail time, and there are several of those, but he never rolled on his partner. Looks like our man likes to be taken care of because in the report there's a list of scorned women who contacted the authorities after he loved them and left them with less than they had before he showed up. It's funny, but from some of the remarks it looks like a few of them would take him back in a minute."

She felt her face flush. "Is he considered dangerous?"

"We know that he has a gun because you saw it. But there is nothing on his record that says he's ever used it in any of the things he's been convicted of. There were a lot of more serious crimes committed that the authorities saw a characteristic operating pattern, but they could never prove it. But, if he really is our ATM robber, we'd have him because the victims reported that they'd been robbed by a gun-wielding man. The problem with that is since none of them ever got a good look at him, we have nothing to work with."

"Do you think it's safe for me to go back to my old apartment? I'm really an intruder here. I'm sure my boss and his mother would like their apartment back."

Sgt. Green hesitated. "Are you afraid of him, Addie? Do you think he'd have any reason to hurt you?"

Remembering the thoughtful and tender lover who she'd lived with for months, Addie said, "If you'd turned up a rap sheet that had included violent crimes, I might have a reason to be afraid of him. But you didn't. So no, I don't think I'm in danger. I just can't see him doing something like that."

"Addie, no one is making you stay away from your own apartment. You are free to live anywhere you want, and while I might not agree with you, I have no authority to do anything about it. Personally, I would feel better if you'd stay hidden until we catch the guy, but it's your choice."

Even though it would make it easier for Earl to find her if she moved back home, continuing to live under the same roof with Jim just wasn't fair to him. Where he was spending his evenings she had no idea, but she did know he was staying away from his own apartment because of her.

"Thank you for your concern, Sgt. Green, but I need to go home."

Chapter 59

Addie stepped off the elevator on the sixth floor and stood quietly while she looked around. So much had happened since the last time she'd been here. Staying away had been a good idea, but it was time for her life to get back to normal.

"Addie! What are you doing here?"

"Oh, hi Jim. Would you believe I've missed this place?"

"For heaven's sake! Are you crazy? That man is probably still looking for you! What are you thinking?!"

"Could we go into your office? I'd like to tell you what I'm thinking."

Explaining to him that she was moving back to her own apartment was difficult because she couldn't tell him the real reason. It just wasn't fair to him if her being there was causing him exquisite pain, as his mother had described it.

Jim listened, and then he said in a resigned voice. "If that's what you want to do, I can't stop you. You might think that Earl wouldn't hurt you, but are you really sure of that?"

"His rap sheet didn't include any violent crimes. If it had, I wouldn't consider leaving your apartment. But it doesn't, so I'm going to take my chances."

"Will you be coming back to work, then?"

"I sure am, and I'm looking forward to it. I'll start Monday morning."

"Come on then. I'll walk you out."

Stepping out the lobby door to the sidewalk, the two of them stopped and shook hands before she turned and walked away.

Addie didn't turn around to see if Jim was watching her.

Why couldn't she fall for a good guy? Not only was Jim the best man she'd ever met, he was as beautiful on the inside as he was on the outside. Now she had to go to his apartment, gather her things and go home. She'd blushed when Sgt. Green had mentioned that some of the women he'd scorned would take him back if they had the chance. Her head knew Earl was nothing but a phony conman, but her heart hadn't been convinced. Maybe if she knew the reason why he had hooked up with her in the first place, it would make a difference.

Neither of them had seen the bald-headed-pot-gutted man on the other side of the street.

*****

His shaved head was sporting a five-o'clock shadow, his padded belly was making him sweat, and the cheek implants were rubbing his tongue. Across the street from Addie's work place, Earl squirmed in discomfort as he waited for the six-o'clock rush of workers to exit her building.

He had almost convinced himself that it was never going to happen. The only hope he had that she was still in the area was that her apartment hadn't changed renters; he'd checked.

The closer Ellen came to her due date, the tighter she became with money. After Steve cut up her credit card, she had very little to give him. Earl could see that source drying up completely after the baby arrived. It wasn't that he didn't have other places to look for help. Already he'd been calling women from his past that he'd escaped from when they discovered what he had been doing to their bank account. Surely he'd find one who could remember all the good times they'd had together and let him come back. So far, he'd gotten nothing but a phone slammed in his ear; he just hadn't contacted the right one.

Six o'clock came, and the door opened. Earl squinted through the brown contact lenses he'd stolen from the Wal-Mart eye center. His vision was a bit blurry; apparently the pair of contact lenses that he'd snatched from a careless shopper were too strong. The constant headache was driving him crazy. He sure would be glad to get rid of them along with the rest of the disguise. It was time to go back to his room and make some more calls.

He was turning to leave when he saw her. Blinking his eyes just to make sure, he saw her stop just outside the door to talk to her boss. After a brief conversation and a handshake, she walked away while the guy just stood and watched her go.

Addie was back! Just the sight of her eased the persistent ache that had become part of him. Would she return to her own apartment now? The thought of being able to talk to her was making his heart pound. All he needed was time alone with her and he'd convince her to take him back. He refused to think about the annoying fact that the law was probably on the lookout for the nonexistent Earl Dixon, and that would mean they couldn't stay around here.

He'd worry about that later.

Chapter 60

Everyone but Ellen thought she was past the due date for her baby to be born. Steve was so edgy expecting to be awakened at any time during the night that he wasn't sleeping well. Every night he rechecked Ellen's overnight case and then placed it back by the door where it had sat for the past two weeks.

She played along with it, knowing quite well that she wasn't nine months pregnant. Of course, her doctor knew, and that was why she'd kept Steve from going with her to her checkups. She'd tried to work the lie into conversations with Steve that there were dark complexioned members in her family tree, but it never went anywhere. Whatever was developing inside her womb, she'd deal with it later. Right now her life was something straight out of the storybooks. With Earl on the lam, he was no longer a threat to her; he had enough problems of his own to keep him busy.

Steve had the car keys in his hand when he stuck his head into the room where she was watching television. "Need anything from the store?" he asked.

"Not that I can think of. Is that where you're going?"

"Yes, I know you can't drink anything alcoholic right now, but I thought I'd buy some champagne so that after the baby comes, you and I can have a drink to toast the addition to our family."

"How sweet!" Ellen felt weepy. "That's such a wonderful thought, Steve."

"Or maybe I should buy wine instead of champagne. I've noticed some local wineries have come out with their own labels."

Ellen's face brightened. "I just remembered! I stuck two bottles of local wine in my closet months ago! I was saving them for your birthday."

"Where in your closet?"

"Behind the ever-growing pile of clothes I've been meaning to take to Goodwill."

"I'll check it," Steve turned and was heading to their bedroom when the doorbell rang.

"Expecting someone?" he asked.

Sweet Adeline

"Remember the couple next to us in our birthing class? I invited them to drop by whenever they were in our neighborhood. Maybe that's who it is."

Steve opened the door, and Ellen heard, "Did we catch you at a bad time?"

"Not at all," she heard Steve reply. "Come on in."

Chapter 61

Addie approached the door of her apartment and wondered what she was going to see when she opened it. Sgt. Green had told her that everything had been taken care of but she wouldn't relax until she saw for herself. He was the one who arranged to have the fingerprinting mess cleaned, her plants watered, and her mail picked up.

A feeling of apprehension made her pause before she turned the key. The apartment would be just as it was that day she'd fled for her life, thinking Earl would try to silence her. Just as the door was about to swing open, strong arms grabbed her from behind and shoved her inside. Once inside, the arms dropped.

"What th—" she yelled.

A familiar voice said quietly, "It's me, Addie. Don't scream."

Whirling around, Addie saw a bald-headed man with brown eyes and a sizable potbelly just staring at her, not touching her and not looking threatening.

Too shocked to speak, she took a step back, intending to run to a room where she could lock the door.

"Don't run. It's me, it's Earl."

She gasped.

And then he chuckled. Her eyes widened in recognition. That was the chuckle that she used to hear when he was teasing her.

"Earl? You scared me to death! And for God's sake, you expect me to recognize you when you look like…like that? "

"Addie, the whole town is looking for me! How else was I going to see you?"

"See me? Earl, you've got to know that things have changed. What makes you think that I want to see you?"

"Don't talk like that! You know you want to see me. You love me!"

"That was before," Addie whispered, and shook her head, "before I found out about you."

"About me? You found something bad about Earl Dixon?" He reached out a hand as if to touch her.

Sweet Adeline

She took another step back. "Earl?" her voice shook. "I really would like for you to stay right where you are. Don't come any closer."

"Aw, Babe, are you really afraid of me?"

She nodded.

"Why would I want to hurt you? I love you, Addie. That's why I'm here. I can't stand being away from you."

There was the sound of regret in her voice when she replied, "I thought I loved you, too."

The disguise made his grin grotesque. "I knew it! We can have it all, Addie! We can be just like we were before...before things went bad for us."

"Not so fast. I've found out who you are, and it has changed how I feel about you."

"You found out who I am? You already know I'm Earl Dixon. What are you talking about?"

"You can stop with the lies. I know you're really Albert Richard Linder, a phony, a thief and a conman."

His eyes showed surprise. "You know? But I thought—"

"I know what you thought. You didn't get rid of all your fingerprints."

Curiosity got the best of him. "Where?"

"In the basement."

When Earl didn't seem to know what she was talking about, she added, "The water pipes."

His shoulders slumped. "Damn. So you know everything?"

She nodded. "That's why I'm surprised that you even dare to show your face around here. Do you think I can still want to see you when I know you for what you really are? A liar, a conman, a thief?"

"Come on! I had to see you! I have to tell you what you've done to me. For the first time in my life, I want to change. I want to be the kind of man that you thought I was!"

"Well you sure messed that up. Now that I know what you are, I could never love you again!"

"Please don't say that! I can't get you out of my head. I...I love you! And I know you feel the same way about me. Addie, you are my last chance. I have never loved anyone before, and for you, I will change."

"Earl, you're pathetic! How can I have this conversation with a paunchy bald-headed man with brown eyes? Even now you're lying! Get rid of the disguise!"

Out came the cheek extenders, and off came the pot gut and the brown contacts. Addie's breath caught in her throat. Standing before her was the man whose dimpled cheeks and fiery blue eyes had captured her heart so many months ago. Her legs were shaking, her mouth was dry, and she felt her resolve melting away. Then she remembered how weak she'd thought those women were that Sgt. Green had talked about.

Straightening her back, she looked at the man who she'd once thought she wanted to marry and realized he no longer had a place in her life. Her legs were still shaking, but her voice was strong. "That's better. Now I can look you in the eye and tell you to get out of my apartment before I call the police. If you go now, I'll wait thirty minutes before I make that call."

"No, no!" There were tears in his sky-blue eyes. "Don't you understand? I'm offering you my love, my life, and I swear, Addie, I'm going to change! I *will* become the man you thought I was. I can do it!"

Taking a deep breath, she steeled herself against the pleading eyes that had so mesmerized her in the past. "Not for me, you won't! Now get out, Earl or Albert or whoever you are! I never want to see you again!"

The look on his face changed. "You feel that way now, but I'm sure I can change your mind. It might take me some time to do it, but I know I can."

"No you can't! Now get out! Go!"

Reaching into his pocket, he pulled out rope and masking tape. Addie watched with unbelieving eyes as he approached her.

"Sorry about this, Addie," he said softly as he grabbed her two hands and wound tape around them. "But I can't let you go. We belong together."

His hand shot out and caught the foot that was headed for his crotch.

"Aw, is this the way it's going to be?" he spoke quietly. "Don't fight me, Honey," he crooned into her ear. "All I ask is for a little time to convince you that we belong together. I hate that I have to do this, but in the end, you'll thank me."

"In your wildest dreams!" She spit in his face.

178

Sweet Adeline

That's when he slapped a piece of tape over her mouth.

*****

Addie woke in the middle of the night in a panic. Why couldn't she move? A simple turn of her head brought her face within six inches of eyes that were staring at her. Because of the tape over her mouth, her scream came out as a muffled moan.

"Awake, Hon?" Earl whispered.

When she tried to jerk away from him, she found that she couldn't move; her hands and her feet were tied to the bed. Sheer terror sent her body into violent spasms.

"Hey, calm down!" he urged. "You're going to hurt yourself!"

The tape over her mouth turned whatever she was yelling into garbled noise.

Pulling her close, he curled his body around her and heaved a contented sigh. "Oh, holding you feels so right! This is what I dreamed about, Addie. You and me, cuddled together like this."

She stiffened her body and struggled to get away from him.

"Now, now, none of that!" he said softly. "Don't fight your love for me. Remember how wonderful it was before...you know what I mean. It can be that way again, Addie. I'm not giving up on us."

With her arms and feet firmly tied to the bed, no amount of thrashing was accomplishing anything. She quit fighting.

"Now you're being good, and when you come to your senses and admit you still love me, I'll remove the tape from your mouth. Until then, since we have a few hours before dawn, let's just go back to sleep." With that, he pulled her even closer and closed his eyes.

Afraid to close hers, she laid wide-awake next to a peacefully sleeping Earl. Tomorrow would be Saturday, the beginning of a weekend.

No one would miss her.

Chapter 62

The manicurist checked her customer's bright red nails, shook her head, and motioned for her to stick her hands back under the light for a few more minutes. "Still a bit tacky," she said. "Three more minutes should do it."

Millie Weber sighed. Just sitting doing nothing was almost impossible for her to do. When she watched television, she knitted. While she waited for the water to boil, she mended. If idle hands are the devil's workshop, then the devil never got any work done in Millie's house.

Three more minutes of sitting absolutely still was making her squirm. When she noticed a man in the waiting area holding up a newspaper while reading it, she knew her problem of what to do for the remaining time was solved; she could read the headings of the articles on the back of his newspaper.

SHOTS FIRED DURING FIGHT OVER TELEVISION. Not being able to read the small print, she couldn't see if anyone was killed by the shot. BOY, 3, FOUND WANDERING IN COMPLEX. Where was the kid's mother? MOSQUITOES STIR UP BUZZ ABOUT WEST NILE. Better put mosquito repellent on her grocery list. MURDER OF JOGGER STILL NOT SOLVED.

That one stopped her cold.

Why hadn't the police paid any attention to her description of the cyclist who'd ridden by the victim once, and then had returned to ride by much slower the second time? Arresting the husband had been so much easier than trying to find the woman on the bicycle. It was a sin what they'd put the poor husband through. Having his wife murdered was horrible enough without him being falsely accused of killing her. In the meantime, the murderer was running around free as a bird. There for a while, she had kept an eye open, hoping to see the woman again, but maybe she was as lazy as the local police; she hadn't done that for months.

The three minutes were up. Millie gathered her purse and the nail polish she'd bought for touch-ups and was preparing to leave when a very pregnant woman pushed her aside and rushed out the door. Millie got a good look at her when she passed outside by the shop's big window. It was the cyclist!

Millie rushed to the receptionist's desk to wait in line behind a woman who was making a future appointment but couldn't remember the date of her husband's office party. Of course that involved a call to her husband to get the correct date, and then the big discussion about whether a morning or an afternoon appointment was best.

Millie was at the exploding point by the time it was her turn. "That pregnant woman who just ran out of here? Do you know her?"

"Wasn't she the rude one?" the receptionist rolled her eyes. "I have no idea who she is."

"Did she make an appointment? I need her name."

"No, she wanted a manicure right now. Silly woman! We're booked weeks ahead, as you know."

Millie's shoulders slumped. "Thanks anyway," she said and left the shop.

Once in her car, she used her cell to make a call.

"Sgt. Green? This is Millie Weber. Remember me?"

"I sure do. How can I help you?"

"It's the other way around, Sergeant. I think I can help you. I just saw the bicycle woman! I don't have her name, but now you can add something to my description of her. The woman looks to be about nine months pregnant! She should be easy to find because there can't be that many women around here about to give birth."

"Millie, thank you so much for the information. I'm on it! I'll be in touch."

She made one stop on the way home to buy mosquito repellent. Feeling good about sharing information that might solve a murder, she sang along with the radio commercial about a tooth-whitening product. Smiling at herself in the rearview mirror, she wondered if maybe she should put the whitener on her next shopping list. There was no such thing as too-white teeth.

Chapter 63

Addie was so hungry her stomach hurt. A few cans of tuna and baked beans that had been in her pantry were now gone; the shelves were empty. Sgt. Green, or maybe someone he hired, had cleaned out all the perishables from her refrigerator when it became apparent that Earl wasn't that easy to find and she wouldn't be coming home. But now she was home, tied to the bed, and with nothing left on her pantry shelf, the chance of alleviating her hunger was nonexistent. Earl had no money, and Addie's purse was nowhere to be found.

"How in hell could you lose your purse?"

"My cell phone is in it, so I sure didn't lose it on purpose! It must be back in…uh, it must be back at the place where I was living."

"Stupid woman! So I'll ask again; where were you living?"

"You can ask me that all you want, and my answer will never change. It's none of your business!"

Two long strides brought him to the side of the bed. Was he going to hit her?

No longer was Earl talking sweet nothings. Because things weren't going the way he thought they would, she could almost see the negative energy radiating off him. By now, she should be loving him the way she had back before things fell apart. But that wasn't happening, and it scared her to think what he might do to her when he finally realized that he'd created a situation that was not going to have a good ending.

Early in the game he'd gone into the bathroom to make a call on his cell phone. Straining her ears, she could hear nothing but muted mumbling except for one phrase. He must have been really upset because when he yelled "Ellen, be reasonable!" the sound had made it out of the bathroom. Ellen? Steve had married an Ellen. It was a common name, but there was no way Earl could know Steve's wife.

Bathroom trips were embarrassing but necessary. At first he'd yelled, "Hold it!", but when she threatened to relieve herself on the bed, he gave in. And that's when the gun appeared. Untying her hands and feet, he pointed it at her until she disappeared inside the bathroom; he was waiting for her when she finished to escort her back to bed.

By Sunday evening, hunger was rearing its ugly head when they were saved by a knock on the door. No words were spoken to whomever it was who'd knocked, but when Earl closed the door, he was carrying a big grocery bag that had the top of a loaf of bread sticking out. Had the mysterious Ellen delivered food?

Afraid to say anything, her empty stomach hurt and her mouth watered while she watched Earl stuff food into his mouth. Tears ran down her cheeks when she realized that he was not going to share. The only thing she could do was to turn her head away from the scene and try to not listen to the sound of his chewing.

She must have dozed off, because the next thing she became aware of was Earl standing next to the bed with a peanut butter sandwich in his hand. He even freed one of her arms so she could feed herself.

She savored every bite.

*****

Addie was counting the hours until Monday morning when the second hand on the clock hit twelve and she wasn't at her desk. Jim would know immediately that something was wrong. He was going to save her.

Chapter 64

James Allen Lawson the Third couldn't believe it. He stood in the presence of James Allen Lawson the Second and realized it was like looking at his own reflection in a mirror.

James the Second was having trouble breathing. This was his son. Stubborn pride had kept him from acknowledging Beth and his child because she had embarrassed him in the eyes of society when she'd left him just weeks after an elaborate wedding. Snide remarks about his not being able to satisfy her in the bedroom had made the rounds. He was the only one who knew that he loved Beth dearly, and when she stormed out of their house, his heart had been broken. She hadn't believed him when he insisted that the whole thing with the live-in maid had been nothing but a big mistake. He really thought she'd come back, but she didn't.

The three wives who followed were mere fill-ins; none of them held a candle to Beth.

*****

Jim watched many emotions flash across his dad's face while he was wondering how to greet the man who hadn't acknowledged his existence until just recently. Do you shake his hand, or do you hug him?

His father solved the problem by grabbing him in a bear hug. Feeling his dad's whole body shaking surprised Jim, and so did the wet tears that he felt on his neck.

It was an emergency in his wife's family that had prompted the trip from the yacht to northern Michigan and the chance to meet the son who was keeping his magazine afloat. He hadn't expected it to be an emotional meeting.

James finally pulled away, pretended that his cheeks weren't wet, and said, "It's nice to finally meet you, Son."

Jim's eyes filled with unshed tears. His dad had called him Son.

The two were staying in a hotel near the hospital where his wife's mother was being treated for a broken hip.

Jim had made arrangements to be away from the office for the next three days. He'd meant to inform Addie, but in his anticipation of seeing his father, he hadn't done it. Anyhow, she'd find out Monday morning when she showed up for work.

Chapter 65

Monday morning couldn't come soon enough. Addie pictured her office with her fellow workers all at their desks by the stroke of nine o'clock. Jim was certain to notice her empty chair. That's when he'd figure out that something was wrong. He would, wouldn't he? He had to! There was no one else to rescue her.

All day Monday she was edgy, waiting and listening. Would Jim just ring her doorbell? He probably thought she was ill and just hadn't felt like calling the office to say she wasn't coming to work. Knowing Earl had a gun, she was scared for Jim's life.

Since her eyes were closed, Earl probably thought she was sleeping, but in reality she was sending mental messages to Jim: Don't ring the doorbell. Don't ring the doorbell. She'd never forgive herself if her relationship with Earl caused something bad to happen to Jim.

Tuesday morning she waited until the clock showed nine o'clock before she allowed herself to hope again. The day began and the day ended; no one came to rescue her.

By Wednesday she resigned herself to the fact that she was on her own. Whoever had brought the food Sunday never showed up again and the pangs of hunger were getting stronger.

Earl wasn't talking, and that was scarier than listening to his threats. His one attempt to make love to her had so sickened her, she'd gagged, which was hard to do with her mouth tapped shut. True, there wasn't anything in her stomach to bring up, but her gag reflex spoke volumes. No longer did Earl have illusions that he could make her love him.

But he was stuck, unable to find a way to escape. The first thing he thought of was her car, but a quick check showed the gas gauge with the needle on empty, the police had towed his stolen car away, and they didn't have a dime between them. Since he had no way to recharge his cell, he used a bit of what he had left to make one last call to Ellen. She hadn't picked up. Too bad Addie didn't have a landline phone.

He was ready to blow the whole failed attempt to win Addie back.

Chapter 66

Steve was puzzled. Why was he the only one who was concerned that Ellen was almost four weeks past her due date? She just waved away his worry every time he brought it up. "First babies come whenever they want," she'd say to him. "Any doctor will tell you that."

That was the reason he was waiting for his name to be called in her doctor's waiting room. Being surrounded by pregnant women was making him extremely uncomfortable. He watched the women when the nurse came out to call in the next patient. To him, they all looked like sedated cows as they studied the one whose name was called as she attempted to get out of her chair. Being the only male in the room, he probably should have at least offered his hand, but he hadn't.

At last, the nurse called his name. This was going to be a short meeting. Just a quick question, a quick answer, and he would be out of here in a matter of minutes.

*****

Dazed, confused and angry, Steve rushed out of the building a half-hour later with murder in his heart. Dr. Brown had tried to calm him down, but the doctor had admitted that if he were in Steve's shoes, he wouldn't want to be calmed down either.

What was he going to do with the information he'd just received? Ellen wasn't past due anything; she was right on schedule. The little bitch had gotten pregnant a month after he last had relations with her.

*****

Another pain hit hard. Where was Steve? He must have turned off his phone because all of her frantic messages went to his answering service.

In desperation, she called 911.

It was in the back of the ambulance that Ellen gave birth to a dark complexioned brown-eyed boy with a full head of black hair that came to a point on his forehead.

The birth had been quick and uncomplicated, and the placenta passed with no problem. This was fortunate because most of the available medical personnel had been dispatched elsewhere to a messy four-car collision. Only one medic was available when Ellen's 911 call came in.

She was holding the alien-looking child wondering who in the world she had picked up that night at Joe's when the conversation between the driver and the medic sitting in the passenger seat got her attention.

"Should we call this one in?"

"Yeah, we should. She sure fits the description of the pregnant biker. Do you have your cell phone with you? Might as well do it now."

"I forgot it. It's back on my desk."

Ellen froze. It was apparent that they didn't know that the panel that separated the cab from the back of the ambulance wasn't closed. She was listening to a conversation that she wasn't supposed to hear. But had she heard right? Earl had said there were witnesses who could describe the cyclist who had been in the neighborhood at the time of the jogger's murder. They were talking about her, but how did they know she was pregnant?

Quickly, she gathered her purse and her cell phone, ready to run at the first opportunity. The baby, who the medic had mostly cleaned, was seriously going to complicate things. Maybe she should leave him behind. She looked down at the strange looking little thing who was rooting around, searching for her breast and hesitated before she slipped her blouse open, not being sure she wanted to do this mother bit. The thought of leaving the baby behind fled the moment he latched onto her swollen breast.

The ambulance pulled into the emergency entrance at the hospital. "Wonder why no one is here to meet us?" the driver grumbled. "I radioed in that I was arriving with a mother and a newborn."

"I'll run inside and tell them that they need to come out and get her and the baby, and then I'll call the police about the cyclist."

"Okay."

The driver was humming, tapping his finger on the steering wheel in time to his song, unaware of what was going on behind him.

This was it, her one opportunity. Mess this up, and her life was over. Frantically, she searched her area looking for anything to help her escape. Her eyes landed on a piece of medical equipment that looked heavy enough to do serious damage.

The baby complained when she pulled him away from her breast. "Be quiet, little guy. I'll be right back," she whispered.

It all happened so fast, the driver was unable to give any details. All he knew was that when he opened his eyes, he was lying on the ground with a huge bump on his head and the ambulance was gone.

Chapter 67

Earl was watching Addie sleep. How stupid was love?! He'd been so overwhelmed by the strange and wonderful emotion that he allowed it to take away his true identity. It had turned him into a sniveling wimp of a man that he neither liked nor wanted to be. Never again!

The vibration of his cell startled him. The call should better be important because it was probably the last call before all bars disappeared.

"Hello?"

"Earl, this is Ellen. Are you ready to blow this gig?"

"More than ready! What's happening?"

"I'm fleeing the scene. Are you with me?"

"Something bad happen to your paradise?"

"Don't ask questions, just look for an ambulance down the block from Addie's apartment. And you better hurry because I'm not waiting. The police will be here any minute."

"I'm on my way!"

Earl took one last look at Addie's sleeping face and was relieved to realize he felt nothing. Not only was love a pain in the ass, it had made him into someone he didn't like. Grabbing a knife, he slashed the ropes that tied her arms to the bed. When she woke up, she could free herself.

He didn't even look back as he ran out of the apartment and headed for Ellen and the ambulance. As he got close, he could see that she had moved to the passenger side of the cab. That was unusual because Ellen, being the bitch that she was, always insisted on driving.

Opening the driver's door, Earl jumped in, threw the engine into gear, and waited until he'd merged with traffic before he glanced over at her. Whoa! Was she doing what he thought she was doing?

"Really, Ellen?" he asked in an I-don't-believe-this-is-happening voice. "You're breast-feeding a baby?"

Joining the background of normal traffic noise, she could hear the dreaded sound of an approaching police siren.

Sweet Adeline

"Shut up and drive, Earl!"

Chapter 68

Steve broke all speed limits getting home. He was imagining how his hands would feel when they were wrapped around Ellen's neck while he squeezed the air out of her lying lungs. What a low-life trick she had pulled on him and it sickened him to think he had fallen for it. When she told him she was pregnant, he had accepted his responsibility like the good man he considered himself to be. But if Ellen had gotten herself impregnated by some other man in order to keep him in the marriage, did that give him a free "get out of jail" card? It was a slick trick that she'd pulled, and she almost got away with it. He had wondered why she would never allow him to go with her to her checkups with the doctor. Now he knew.

Killing her might make him feel good initially, but in the long run, spending the rest of his life in jail wasn't something he really wanted to do. For that reason, he had to tone down his anger.

Finally, his house was in sight. Why no officer of the law hadn't stopped him for the two red lights he'd run, the stop sign he had ignored, and the speed limit he'd exceeded was truly a miracle.

What was he going to say to her? Did he even owe her a chance to explain? What he wanted to do was order her out of his house. But where could a pregnant woman go?

Steve's mind was in a whirl. Wouldn't the husband of a married couple be considered the father of the baby? If that were true, he could lose his house to Ellen and be forever responsible for her and the kid. Maybe a blood test would get him off the hook. What a mess!

The first thing he noticed as he rushed to the house was that the front door was standing wide-open. Burglars? That possibility brought him to a halt. His good sense told him that he should call the police before he blundered into a dangerous situation.

That's when he noticed that the overnight case that had been right by the door for the last four weeks was gone. A search of the house brought him to the kitchen where he spied a note on the table that said in large black marker letters, "Where the hell are you? I had to call 911!"

Sweet Adeline

Ellen was gone. All the pent-up anger that had built up inside him on the trip from her doctor's office quickly deflated. She was at the hospital having the kid. How was he supposed to act? Should he go to the hospital and hold her hand while she gave birth to a baby that wasn't his?

He needed a drink.

Being a good person, he had done away with all alcoholic beverages in the house because if his wonderful wife, you know, the one who was right now giving birth to a baby that wasn't his, couldn't drink, then neither would he. How naïve! He wanted to puke.

Somewhere in this house there had to be something alcoholic. Oh, yes. There were two bottles of local wine they were going to drink to toast the birth of their child. What a wonderful idea that had been! Ellen had been so touched by his suggestion she'd actually shed a few sweet tears. Just thinking how blindly he'd swallowed the farce caused bitterness to fill his mouth.

Where did Ellen say she'd put them?

It took some hunting, but he eventually found a sack in her closet behind clothes meant for Goodwill. Carrying it to the kitchen, he emptied the bag of its two bottles and the crumpled pieces of paper that had kept them from hitting each other.

The bottles had the names of two different wineries on the labels. While thinking how fortunate it was that the making of wine had taken off so successfully in the cold climate of northern Michigan, he found a corkscrew and opened and sampled both of them.

Feeling a bit more settled, he decided that he would treat the situation like the civilized man that he was. What else could he do? Divorce a woman who had just given birth to a child everyone would think was his?

It was time to go to the hospital and do his thing. The wine was good and should be refrigerated, so he proceeded to tidy the kitchen. It was when he picked up the pieces of paper that the official lettering on one of them caught his eye. When he smoothed it out, he saw that it was a marriage certificate of a guy named Albert Richard Linder and a woman named El...whoa! Ellen Joyce Short. Short was his wife's maiden name.

It took him a few seconds to realize what he was holding in his hand. Ellen had married a guy by the name of Albert and never mentioned it? And how in the hell had the certificate ended up in the wine sack? She obviously hadn't known it was there; no way would she have allowed such a damning piece of information anywhere near him. So who had put it there?

But if the certificate were real, then Ellen was a bigamist. That would mean that when they'd run into each other at the high school reunion, she was already a married woman. No, Ellen was too smart to do something as dumb as that. There had to be a divorce record somewhere, or maybe an annulment. Even if there were, it still didn't explain how the marriage certificate had ended up in their closet.

Feeling his knees about to buckle, he found a chair and collapsed. Before he went to the hospital, he had to find out if the certificate was real.

This called for another drink. Opening the refrigerator, he removed one of the bottles, grabbed a clean glass, and poured.

Not being used to alcohol, he was staggering a bit, but he made it to his study without spilling a drop.

Opening up his computer, he went online and made a simple request about marriage certificates. That took him to a site where for $4.95 he would have access to all kinds of records for the next several days. After he charged the fee on his Amazon account, he typed in Ellen Joyce Short and held his breath. In a short period of time, he found his answer. She had married Albert, and since there was no record of either a divorce or an annulment, she was still married to him.

He'd found the solution to his problems.

Chapter 69

For three days, Jim had his dad all to himself. All his boyhood and adult fantasies didn't hold a candle to the real thing. His dad was a kind, considerate, and funny man. Jim was pleasantly surprised because even though his mom had never said a bad word about him, she hadn't had to. Just knowing that she'd left her new husband after a few weeks of marriage spoke volumes about him. Added to that was the fact that two more of his wives had done the same thing.

It was a deep conversation during dinner at a five-star restaurant that the conversation got quite personal. Jim never had any male friends to confide in and boys have a hard time talking to their mother about matters of the heart. But here was his dad, interested enough to ask probing questions.
*****
James was having trouble keeping his emotions under control. Across the table from him sat the son who he'd neglected all the kid's life. He was the loser because he was the one who had missed watching Jimmy grow up. It surprised him how sad he felt that he'd had no hand in turning the boy into the extraordinary man who was seated across the table. His feeling of regret was so strong it was making it hard for him to swallow food.

Because Beth thought he was lying, she had walked away from their marriage after just a few wonderful weeks. Over the years, the last scene replayed itself again and again:
*****
After a night of love, Beth rolled out of bed.

"Hey, Babe! Where do you think you're going? I was planning on spending the whole morning in bed!"

"I was, too, but I just remembered I have to return something to the store."

"Another duplicate wedding gift?"

"Would you believe triplicate? I won't be gone long. I'll ask our driver to double-park while I run into the store. So stay right where you are! I'll surprise you when I return because I intend to crawl right back into bed with you." She threw him a kiss as she ran out of the room.

"I'll miss you desperately, so hurry!"

She laughed, and called back, "Keep the bed warm for me, Honey!"

Later, when he was roused from sleep by the feel of bare warm flesh touching him, he didn't bother to open his eyes. He just responded.

That's how Beth had found him with the live-in maid when she walked into the bedroom.

Why didn't Beth have faith in him? How could she believe that he'd throw away the wonderful thing the two of them had for a casual romp in bed?

He waited for her to return and say that she believed him, but Beth hadn't come back. It was only when she was struggling to stay alive because a difficult pregnancy was making it too hard for her to hold down a job that she'd called him for help. That's when he'd found out that he'd lost more than just a wife; he'd also lost the child she was carrying.

Anger at the shame she'd brought to him and his high-society parents, the family's team of lawyers prepared a divorce decree that set up an alimony amount so punitive, a mother and child could not possibly survive on it.

Beth wanted out of the marriage, so she signed it. Tonight he'd learned that his retaliatory action had forced her to hold down two jobs.

How could he repay his son for the years of struggling that he could so very easily have prevented? From what Jim had said, he and his mother were now living quite comfortably since Jim had taken the job managing his magazine. Other magazines were folding, but *Your World* was thriving. The kid deserved a raise in salary.

"Jim, I'm really enjoying the new feature you added. Dr. Ask-Me-Anything is a riot! Will I have a chance to meet the person who writes it?"

"Only if you can keep a secret," Jim grinned as he answered.

"No one in the office knows who he is?"

"It's a woman."

James raised his black eyebrows. "A woman?"

Sweet Adeline

"Wait until you meet her." Jim looked off into space, and when he looked back, he had a dreamy look in his eye. "She's something special."

"Oh," James laughed. "It's like that, is it?"

"I'd like for it to be, but she doesn't see me that way."

"Is she blind?" his dad asked.

"No, Addie isn't blind. She seems to fall for men who are either inappropriate or dangerous. All she sees when she looks at me is her boss."

"Maybe she just has to get to know you."

"She knows me, Dad. She actually lived with Mom and me for a while. Well, she was actually hiding from her last boyfriend who'd turned out to be a bad apple."

"How interesting! What did Beth say about that?"

"Mom really likes her! You'd have to know how our apartment is laid out to understand how Mom can come and go without running into anyone else who lives there. We really see very little of each other."

"This Addie girl, is she still living with you?"

"She moved back to her own apartment Friday."

"The bad apple isn't around anymore?"

"Who knows? She claimed she wasn't afraid of him anymore and she wanted to go home. I haven't seen her since the move because I've been with you."

"You really like her?"

Jim looked down at the table. "I love her."

"Does she know how you feel about her?"

"How can I make a move when there's always another guy in the picture? This last one, Earl, was movie-star handsome."

"He's the bad apple?"

Jim nodded.

"Do you think she still loves him?"

"Dad, she's scared of him!"

James grinned. "Looks like it's your turn, Son. Just don't hesitate when an opportunity presents itself."

"What if there's no opportunity?"

James paused before he replied. Maybe he could repay his son by sharing information. If only someone had stepped in so many years ago and pointed out the mistakes he was making with Beth. But no one had, and look at the mess he'd made with his life. He hadn't told anyone, but his fourth wife had made it plain that she wasn't going back to the yacht with him.

"Jim I'm going to tell you something. It seems that the Lawson men fall in love only once in their life. At least that's what both my father and I have experienced. Beth was it for me, but being young and stupid, I did something that made her leave. My big mistake was not trying to get her back. The wedding had cost a small fortune, and she had embarrassed me and my family when she left me just a few weeks afterwards. So it was pride that wouldn't allow me to plead with her to come back, and I lost her permanently. And look what else I lost. I lost you, Jimmy, and I'll always regret that."

"But Dad, you moved on! You must have loved again because you married three more women."

"And every one of those women left me because I couldn't love them. Marrying them was a mistake, Jim. Once I'd tasted real love with Beth, no one else could replace her."

"So you still love Mom?"

"More than ever. I'm surprised that she never remarried. Is she still beautiful?"

Jim nodded, "She was a model for years, and now she manages the agency."

"Does she ever talk about me?"

"Never. She wouldn't even show me a picture of you, so I had no idea what you looked like. I did go online and looked up 'widow's peak' and found that it's an inherited trait. Figured it must have been from you since Mom's side doesn't have any."

"So many years wasted!" James reached over and touched Jim's hand. "Did you listen to what I told you about the Lawson men loving just one woman? I hope you did, because if this Addie is the one you've chosen, don't let her get away."

"I don't know what else to do, Dad. It seems like it's never my turn with her."

"Let's call it a night. I want to get up early tomorrow because I intend to go back with you. I need to see the crew that produces *Your World*, and I especially want to meet Addie."

Chapter 70

Addie slowly opened her eyes. Not wanting Earl to know she was awake, she moved nothing but her eyes.

He wasn't in her bed, he wasn't in her kitchen, and if he were in the bathroom, he wasn't making any noise. Feeling a sneeze coming on, her hand automatically flew to her mouth to cover it. Her hand. It was free! In fact, the rope on both hands had been cut.

The first thing she did was rip the tape off her mouth. Skin came off with it, but the relief of having it gone diminished the pain. Untying her feet was the second thing she did. The third was picking up and unplugging the bedside lamp to use as a club on the son-of-a-bitch who had kept her captive for seven days.

Her bravery and good intentions faltered when her feet hit the floor. All those days of inactivity had weakened her; her legs collapsed and she fell.

If Earl heard that, he was going to be flying out of the bathroom in a matter of seconds and find that she was free.

Afraid to breathe, she stayed on the floor and waited.

Nothing happened.

Not trusting her legs, she crawled on her hands and knees to the bathroom, and then with all the nerve she had left, she pushed open the door. The room was empty.

Earl was gone.

She had tried to keep track of the days and she didn't know if she was right, but she'd eaten her last bite of food on Tuesday and that was two mornings ago. Today was Thursday.

How could Jim not miss her? Anyone who wasn't at their desk by nine o'clock in the morning had to answer Jim's phone call. Her purse and her cell phone were probably still in his condo so even if he had called, no one would have heard it ring. Was he angry at her for not answering her phone, or maybe because she moved out? Or perhaps he just had given up trying to make her think of him as someone other than her boss and decided not to have anything more to do with her.

That thought brought her to tears. Why had she wasted her time on losers like Steve and Earl when Jim had been right there, waiting for her to notice him?

Pulling herself off the floor by holding on to the doorframe, she staggered to her front door and locked it. Her steps were quite steady by the time she finished setting the two locks on the back door. If Earl intended to come back, he was going to have trouble getting in.

On the way through the kitchen, she stopped at the sink and drank several glasses of water. Feeling a bit better, she headed to the bathroom to turn on the hot water in the shower. That's when she noticed the scales. It seemed eons ago since she'd weighed herself. The last time was after her three days of mourning her loss of Steve. What a fiasco that had been!

Turning her face towards the flow of water, she stood in the shower and imagined every trace of Earl on her body was being washed down the drain. The hot water finally ran out and the cold water chased her out of the shower. The whole process had worn her out, so after dressing, she looked at the bed she'd been tied to for seven days and shook her head. No way was she crawling back in there until she changed the bedding.

Food. She needed food. A car with an empty gas tank, and without a dime to her name, she pondered her next step. During the Steve days, she'd been on diets when she'd fasted for two days, so as long as she drank enough water, she knew she was going to be alright.

She spent the next hour knocking on her neighbors' doors. Most of them didn't answer because they were at work, and the ones who did were usually children who'd been left alone and told not to talk to strangers. No one allowed her to use their phone.

She returned home even hungrier than she was before she started out. She had to do something, but what? She looked at the bed again, shook her head, and stretched out on the floor. After a little nap, she'd figure out something.

Where the hell was Jim?

Chapter 71

Jim was proud of his crew. They had no idea that their boss was back, but when he and his dad stepped into the front office, every one of his employees was busy working. In fact, no one even noticed that they had visitors.

"I'm impressed," James said. "You must be an excellent manager."

Jim glowed.

"Now, where is this Addie woman? You said she was a redhead, but I don't see one."

"She is right over th—" Jim stopped talking. Addie's chair was vacant.

When he clapped his hands together, every worker looked up, and every worker smiled a greeting to their boss.

"Why is Addie not at her desk?"

He was met with puzzled faces. One worker spoke up. "She hasn't been at her desk for weeks! Don't you remember telling us she had a family emergency and wouldn't be back until it was over?"

Only he knew that she'd left his place on Friday and expected to be back to work on Monday. That was four days ago.

"Oh, no!" Jim exclaimed.

"Something wrong?"

"Something's terribly wrong. Addie's in trouble."

*****

It was a short trip to her apartment and within minutes, both men were rattling her apartment door, ringing her doorbell and shouting her name.

"What the hell is going on?" a man's gruff voice called.

"Where's the apartment manager?" Jim yelled. "We need to get inside."

"And why would that be?" the man asked.

"We think something bad has happened to the woman who lives here. No one has seen her since Friday."

"Oh, that's Miss Addie's apartment. Who would want to harm her? I call her Sweet Adeline, you know." As he chuckled, he pulled a ring of keys out of his pocket and unlocked her door. "I'm the guy you're looking for."

The open door revealed Addie lying face down on the floor. "Dad, call the police!"

Rushing into the room, he knelt and touched her. "Oh, God! Addie, can you hear me?"

*****

Terrified, Addie woke up when she felt a hand touching her. Earl was back!

Swinging her fist with all the strength she had left, she connected with something. "Take your filthy hands off me!" she roared.

Jim fell back, surprised by the punch on his chin.

"Well, she's not dead!" he heard his dad say.

"Oh, it's you, Jim," she cried. "I thought you were Earl."

"He found you?" Jim asked as he helped her to her feet.

"Oh, Jim," her voice cracked, "That bastard grabbed me when I came home on Friday."

Jim held his breath. "Did he…did he—"

Addie shook her head. "No, nothing like that. He didn't hurt me, just tied me up and kept trying to convince me to take him back – like I'd even consider that after what he did!"

"So where is he now?"

"All I know is that when I woke up, my hands were free and he was gone."

"Gone?"

"He had no money and no bars left on his phone, so I have no idea where he went."

Jim desperately wanted to gather her into his arms, but he hesitated. What if she didn't want that? Could he stand being rejected while his father watched?

James observed his son's indecision. Hadn't he listened to anything he'd said?

"Son, it's your turn."

The thought that maybe it just might be his turn gave Jim the courage to do what he'd been dreaming about since the first day he'd laid eyes on her. He kissed her.

Addie's green eyes looked into brown love-filled ones. Jim had finally come; she was safe.

Sweet Adeline

It never entered her mind that she'd just been kissed by her boss. Instead, she was consumed by the feeling that this handsome and truly honorable guy was someone so much more. Reaching up, she pulled his head down, looked him in the eye, and said, "I knew you would rescue me, Jimmy! But what took you so long?"

And then she kissed him.

When James cleared his throat, Addie's eyes landed on a man who was almost an exact replica of Jim.

"Your dad?" she asked.

"Yes, I finally got to meet him. That's where I've been."

James looked at the green-eyed girl that had captured his son's heart. "Hello, Addie. I'm very glad to meet you." Turning to Jim, he spoke in a low voice. "She probably should be looked at by a doctor. I think you should call an ambulance."

Addie protested loudly. "No, I don't need an ambulance! I just need to eat something! I'm starved!"

James pulled out his cell.

"I'm going to be fine!" she repeated as she tried to grab the phone out of his hand.

Jim held her in his arms while James dialed 911.

"No, you're not fine! Oh, the police are here."

Jim opened the door and Sgt. Green rushed in.

Before he could say a word, Addie exclaimed, "Don't you dare say, 'I told you so!'"

Sgt. Green dropped the finger he was prepared to point at her. It was unusual for someone to talk to him that way, but Addie was a special case. "Did he hurt you?" he asked quietly.

"Being tied to the bed wasn't comfortable, but no, he never hurt me. We both suffered from lack of food."

Jim stepped in. "I'm Jim Lawson, and that's my dad."

Sgt. Green nodded his head. "You're the guy Addie was staying with?"

Jim nodded, "Until Friday, and then she wanted to come home."

"She should have stayed with you." Sgt. Green couldn't help himself.

Addie cleared her throat.

"Okay." He threw up his hands. "I get it, but you're lucky that Earl, or whatever he's calling himself now, didn't hurt you. Did he mention why he was conning you?"

Jim's black eyebrows shot up.

"I tried, but with tape over my mouth he couldn't understand what I was asking."

"May I ask what the question was?" Jim inquired.

Addie nodded. "What reason did he have to con me? Believe me, he planned the two *accidental* times he ran into me. Something else was going on, but for the life of me, I can't figure out what it was. Maybe I'll never know."

When they heard the sound of a vehicle pulling up to the apartment, Jim turned to the officer. "The ambulance is here to take Addie in for observation. She doesn't want to go, but seven days of being held captive, she really should get checked out."

"I'll follow the ambulance, and after she's checked in, I'll take her statement."

"Quit talking as if I'm not here!" she complained.

"She's a feisty one, isn't she?" Sgt. Green observed.

Chapter 72

Addie woke up to the clattering sound of the food cart coming down the hall. Must be lunch-time. So much had happened it was hard to believe it was just noon. The broth and Jello she'd eaten upon her admittance hadn't come close to satisfying her need for real food.

She heard paper rustling and her eyes traveled to Jim who looked uncomfortable sitting in the straight-back chair by her bed. He hadn't left her side for a minute since he'd found her this morning. Throughout the whole admittance procedure, he'd taken over in a gentle but forceful way. While he didn't fuss over her, she couldn't remember when she'd felt so safe. His voice, his eyes and his actions were so filled with care, she felt as if a soft blanket of love covered her.

There weren't many men in her life to compare him with. Steve had been full of himself, and as she looked back on the years with him, she realized that she never had been first in his priorities. Maybe that's why he had been able to walk away so thoughtlessly, and why getting over him had been rather easy. Earl had been exciting, sometimes making her feel as if she were playing with fire. Apparently, she had been.

But Jim. She'd known almost from the beginning that her boss had feelings for her. But except for the birthday cake incident and his asking her out to dinner, he hadn't stepped out of line, not even when she told him that Steve had married someone else. If Earl hadn't come along when he did, she was pretty sure that Jim would have made his move. But Earl had come along, and dazzled by his good looks and charm, she'd latched onto him thinking that she was the luckiest woman in the world.

With Jim, the world wasn't filled with fireworks. It was filled with the calm and contented feeling that comes when you watch a beautiful sunset, a feeling that Addie hadn't even known what she was looking for until it found her. Steve had been a spark, and Earl had been a blazing bonfire. Now she realized that what she wanted was that warm, slow burn of a fire in the hearth.

"Looks like lunch is here," Jim said as he folded up the newspaper he was reading. "You hungry?"

"Starved! The Jello and broth weren't real food. I don't think I'll ever be full again," she mused.

Small portions of easy-to-digest food looked like a Thanksgiving feast to Addie, but as her mother always said, some days her eyes could be bigger than her stomach. And today was no exception.

Halfway through her meager lunch, she pushed the tray away.

"I thought you said you'd never be full again," Jim teased.

Addie picked at her fingernails, not looking up. "I didn't think I would be. I swear sometimes I could even smell something cooking, and I'd wake up and—" Addie paused, hugging herself. "He would just be staring at me."

She closed her eyes and shuddered as tears slowly leaked out of the corners of her eyes.

Jim didn't say a word. He just got up from his chair, kicked off his shoes, crawled in beside her, and gathered her shaking body close.

That's how Sgt. Green found them when he entered Addie's room to take her statement.

Chapter 73

Jim burst into the front office waving the latest issue of *Your World*, still warm from the press.

"We have another winner!" he proudly announced to his crew.

"I want to see it!"

Several writers actually tried to grab the magazine out of his hand. He laughed as he headed for the safety of his office. "Be patient! The printer is sending up one for each of you. This one's mine to gloat over."

Jim was laughing a lot these days. It thrilled him to catch Addie giggling or blushing when he looked at her. He was pretty sure that most of the *Your World* crew had figured it out. It still amazed him that it really might be his turn.

A brief knock on his door warned him before the door opened and his dad stepped in.

"Morning, Dad. I'm surprised to see you here. I thought you'd be back on the yacht by now."

"I thought so, too, but I've been thinking—"

"Oh, oh. Sounds like trouble's coming for someone," Jim chuckled.

"You never met Cora, my fourth wife," James paused to make a face. "That sounds horrible, doesn't it? *My fourth wife*. Well, I can't talk her into going back to the yacht with me. And I can't blame her. Life on the Mediterranean might sound glamorous, but it's not. Between entertaining guests and throwing parties there are a lot of lonely days. If I were more of a companion, there wouldn't be a problem, but according to Cora, I'm not."

"Have a seat, Dad."

James sat down. "Remember I told you that Lawson men only fall in love once in their life? Well, Beth was it for me. I'm still young with a lot of life left to live, and I don't want to be alone for the rest of it. But if I married again, I'm sure it would just end up just like the others."

*****

"This is what you're thinking about instead of going back to your yacht?"

"Yes. I made you and your mother's life harder than it should have been when she was raising you. I always had money, and then when my dad died, he left me more money than I can spend in my lifetime. I was so heartbroken and angry when Beth left, I intentionally didn't give her enough to live on. I secretly thought it might make her come back."

"Dad, Mom and I did okay. She's pretty spectacular, you know."

James nodded, "I know. Before I ask, I need to know if she has ever had a serious relationship…that you know of."

Jim looked puzzled. "I don't know the answer to that. I don't think she'd even discuss something like that with me."

"So there never was a man hanging around your apartment?"

"No, but Mom comes and goes as she pleases. The way our apartment is laid out, we don't see each other very often. Dad, where is this conversation going?"

"Do you think Beth would consider meeting me for a drink? We haven't spoken to each other since the night she caught me with—" James' hand flew to cover his mouth.

Jim's eyes widened. "I've never heard this part of the story. She caught you with someone? You had just been married!"

James hung his head. "It was all a big misunderstanding and when she chose not to believe my explanation, she swung her fist and hit me." His chuckle was dry. "My nose bled like a stuck pig."

"There has to be more to the story!" Jim insisted.

"There is, but now is not the time for stories."

Jim looked disappointed, but for the time being, he'd wait to hear it later. "So because you can't seem to settle for any other woman, you want to see if Mom will take you back?"

"I know it's a crazy idea, but I'm not going anywhere until I find out. After all, Beth hasn't found anyone, either."

"No, but she was busy raising a kid and working like a dog," Jim snapped.

His father didn't seem to hear him. He was smiling to himself. "Maybe I'm not the only one who loves only once. Could it be that we were a matched pair from the beginning?"

208

"If you were, you sure shot the hell out of that in short order." Jim sounded disgusted.

"Don't think I haven't paid! The amount of alimony I shell out to my exes could run a small country. But money isn't what's important," James said softly. "The hole in my heart is."

Jim narrowed his eyes and studied his father. Should he help his dad who, until recently, hadn't given him the time of day, or should he stay loyal to his mom? She was angry enough to leave James, but when he was born, she still had named him after his dad. Did that mean she had feelings for him? What if his mother still loved James even after what he'd done to her?

"On the chance that mom is carrying a torch for you, I'll help. Do you want the meeting to be arranged, or would you rather run into her by a well-planned accident?"

"It would be too easy for her to turn down a scheduled meeting, so let's go for the well-planned accident. Is there something that the two of you do together on a regular basis?"

Jim thought. "Ever since you gave me the job of managing *Your World*, we've been having breakfast at the end of each month to go over the bills and split them. It's kind of a celebration for me to be able to pitch in and help. Until you hired me, Mom was doing it all by herself."

James flinched, but recovered quickly. "Where do you go for breakfast?"

"Mom still watches what she eats, but once a month she sure enjoys The House of Pancakes. We're meeting there at eight o'clock this Friday."

The thought of seeing Beth again was making James's heart pound. If nothing else came from the meeting, he at least would have a chance to beg her forgiveness for what had happened.

"How good of an actor are you?" James asked.

Jim looked surprised. "What kind of a question is that?"

"I expect you to win an Oscar for your surprised reaction when I accidentally bump into the two of you Friday morning."

After his dad left, Jim was having second thoughts about what he'd just done. If his mom ever found out that he was part of the plan, would she feel like her own son had betrayed her? They had been a team when things got tough and money was tight, and here he was, siding with the enemy. He could always suggest a change of restaurants, or even a change of time. It wouldn't be hard to come up with some excuse to do either of those things and his mother would never suspect a thing. It had happened before.

Yes, he'd pick a change of time and James would be out of the picture.

A tap on the door interrupted his daydream. Since he'd been busy all morning with the printing of the new issue, he hadn't had a chance to talk to Addie. In fact, putting the magazine together had kept him busy for the past couple of days. Hoping it was Addie who was tapping on his door, he called, "Come in."

He was shocked at the sight of her standing in front of his desk. Makeup almost but not quite hid the dark circles under her bloodshot eyes.

"Addie, what's wrong. Are you feeling okay?"

She shook her head.

"Talk to me!"

"I was wrong when I insisted on going back to my own apartment."

Jim opened his mouth to say something but she stopped him.

"Please don't say 'I told you so.'"

The expression on his face changed. "Did Earl…?"

"No, he didn't come back. It's me," she lowered her eyes. "I can't stand the thought of sleeping in bed even though I've changed all the bedding. It's not just the bed, because I can't sleep anywhere in the apartment. Jim, all I can think about is how safe I felt when you crawled into my hospital bed and held me. I need you."

Jim swallowed hard. The woman he'd loved for years just said she needed him. Needed him for what? For her, what she remembered about the night at the hospital was the feeling of being safe. For him, it had been so much more than that. He should be ecstatic that she wanted him in her bed, but his good common sense held him back. If she needed him just because she was scared, that was not enough. She had to need him because she loved him, and he was not settling for anything less.

"The offer is still open to come back and live with mom and me. Why don't we move your things after work today? You can have your old room back."

Addie looked disappointed.

"Something wrong?" he asked.

"I…I…I was thinking I'd be moving into your room."

Sweet Adeline

Jim's inner voice kept repeating, *be strong, be strong.* "No, Addie, it's much too soon to be moving into my room. Our relationship isn't ready for that yet."

She looked alarmed. "But I thought…I thought—"

"It's not that I wouldn't love to have you in my bed, because believe me, that's been my dream for a long time."

Addie's face turned red as she realized what she'd done. For the sake of feeling safe, she'd offered her body as payment. Knowing that there was a word that defined what that made her, she turned to leave.

"Wait. Don't go," he pleaded.

Unable to meet his eyes, she looked at the floor. "I've ruined it, haven't I?"

"Ruined what?"

"Ruined your opinion of me. You deserve someone who has higher moral standards than I have."

"Stop talking like that! I'm very aware of your past. Hell, suffering through Steve was bad, but that thing you had with Earl almost destroyed me! Addie, I'm no angel. I have a past, too, but I want something different for us."

"Different?"

"My feelings for you are strong because I've had them for so long. If you do have any for me, they're too new to be deep. Addie, I want this thing between us to have a good foundation before we jump into something as life-changing as sleeping together."

Her mouth dropped open. Jim wanted more than sex. He was taking their relationship to a higher level.

Jim sat unmoving at his desk, his face full of apprehension as he waited for her to say something.

Was she ready for something more?

Her whole body relaxed. Reaching across his desk, she laid her hand on the side of his face. "Jim, that's the most wonderful thing any man has ever said to me."

Taking her hand off his face, he squeezed it. "You game to stick with me and see what happens?"

"More than ever!"

"Good! I'll help you move your things after work today."

She was smiling when she left his office.

Chapter 74

It was Friday morning and Jim was nervous. In a few hours, he would be meeting his mother at The House of Pancakes. What would happen when his dad showed up was giving him a bad case of the jitters. He'd decided not to change the time.

When he entered the kitchen, he saw that Addie was already at the table reading the morning paper and drinking coffee.

"Anything interesting?" he asked while trying to pour coffee with a shaking hand.

"Good morning, and yes, there is something *really* interesting in the paper. It seems that an abandoned ambulance was found in Ohio."

"Now, that *is* interesting! Are they thinking it's the one Steve's wife stole?"

"Has to be, because there was a newborn baby left inside it. There's even a picture of it. Here, take a look."

When he leaned over, coffee splashed out of his cup and landed on the baby's face.

"Whoops," he exclaimed. "Sorry about that."

What he missed seeing was a baby that had a dark widow's peak.

"Wonder how Steve's taking the news that his wife is probably the one who murdered the jogger? He'll have to raise the baby all by himself."

"Serves him right," she muttered, scanning the rest of the article.

Her next cry was so loud Jim spilled more of his coffee.

"Really, Addie," he complained. "Now I have to change my shirt."

"Listen to this! It seems that a marriage certificate has surfaced for…for…oh, my God, for an Albert Richard Linder and an Ellen Joyce Short! The only Ellen I know is the one who Steve married. Hey, wait a minute! When Earl was keeping me a prisoner, I heard him talking on his cell to an Ellen, who I think is the one who brought us food. Could it be that Earl and Steve's Ellen are married to each other? That son-of-a-bitch!"

Sweet Adeline

Jim snorted. "You were living with a married man, and if this Ellen is who you think she is, then your old boyfriend is married to a bigamist!"

She flapped the paper at him. "Rub it in!"

He chuckled.

"Maybe that's why he conned me."

"I don't understand."

"I don't either. But Steve was trying to talk me into taking him back after he divorced Ellen. Maybe Earl's job was to get involved with me so that I wouldn't go back to Steve."

"Hmmm. I think that's reaching a bit too far. Why would Earl want to help his wife stay with another man?"

"You're probably right."

"Anything else?"

"Oh, yes there is! The ambulance gave the cops some very good fingerprints. One set belonged to Ellen. The other set belonged to…hey, you wanna guess who?"

Jim pretended to ponder. "Earl? So Earl and Steve's Ellen *are* married! "

"Correct! But the paper calls him Albert. The day he cut my ropes and disappeared, Ellen must have picked him up. Anyhow, there's an all-points bulletin out for the capture of the two of them."

"It's a relief to know Earl's far away in another state. Do you feel safe, now?"

"Enough so that I'm going back to my own apartment after work today."

Jim turned away so that she wouldn't see the disappointed look on his face. "Look at the time! I'll see you at work, Addie. The only thing I have planned today is lunch with mom."

Addie blew him a kiss. "I promise I'll be at my desk and sitting in my chair when the big hand hits twelve."

Chapter 75

"Why are you so fidgety?" Beth asked her son. "You're making me nervous."

"Sorry, Mom. I just have some problems back at the office that I can't stop thinking about."

"Maybe we should have postponed breakfast because we haven't gotten anything…done…"

Jim looked up from the telephone bill he was holding to find out why his mom had stopped talking. What he saw on her face was downright scary. Oh, oh. Showtime.

Standing by their table was James Allen Lawson the Second. Jim froze. Why hadn't he switched the time? His mother was going to kill him if she ever found out he was in on the accidental meeting.

Beth and James stared at each other. Neither spoke. Finally, Beth slowly pushed back her chair and stood up. Jim held his breath when she took a step toward her ex. Was she going to kiss him? James must have thought so because his arms were open and he was smiling.

Jim spent a lot of time at the gym so he knew how to throw a roundhouse punch; apparently so did his mother.

James had to recover from the punch that rocked him back on his heels before he quietly remarked, "You missed my nose."

There was murder in her eye as she pulled back to hit him again. James caught her arm.

"What the hell are you doing here?" she hissed.

"I might ask you the same question," he replied calmly.

"That's a dumb thing to say because I live here and you don't. What's the matter? Your yacht sink?"

"You wish."

"I wish? I don't waste my time thinking about you at all. Now will you please leave? I was having a peaceful breakfast with our son before you rudely interrupted. Oh, would you care for an introduction?"

Jim sat with his mouth open, watching his parents having what might turn out to be the fight of the century. My God, what made him think that getting the two of them together was a good idea? He looked around for the nearest exit in case he needed to get out of here in a hurry.

"You don't have to introduce me to our son because we've already met. In fact, we spent three *delightful* days together. But if you'd like to make a formal introduction, go right ahead. It would really be the polite thing to do, and knowing you, you always know what the right thing is," and then he added sarcastically, "...about everything."

"I'm glad you realize that! Jim, meet your dad. Now run along, James."

James didn't move. "You know what hurts the worst?" he asked softly. "It's the fact that you won't believe me. Beth, what we had was so wonderful! How could you even *think* I'd do anything to jeopardize something as precious as that? But stubborn you, you choose to believe I lied."

"So you're sticking to your story that you thought that the woman who slipped into your bed was me?"

"It's not a story, Beth. It's the truth. Why would I want to change a true story?"

Beth shook her head in disgust.

James threw up his hands. "I give up. You haven't changed. It was nice seeing you again, and Son, I'll talk to you later."

With that, he turned and walked away.

Jim watched his mother fall apart. This was his fault. When she found out, and she probably would, that he'd arranged this little meeting, she might never forgive him.

Watching James leaving was painful. His father's shoulders were slumped and his head was bent, the very picture of dejection. Across the table from him, his mother was sobbing quietly into her hands.

He couldn't help himself. Two people were miserable and they didn't have to be. Whatever happened so many years ago shouldn't be destroying what could be a beautiful thing today.

Reaching across the table, he pried his mother's hands away from her face. "Mom," he said softly. "Are you going to just sit there and let him disappear again?"

"Wh...what?" she sniffed.

Jim picked a napkin off the table and handed it to her. "Guess it's up to me to be the adult in this mess. Wipe your face.

I've spent the last three days with the man you just sent away. He's a good man, and he loves you. Why are you letting him leave?"

By this time, James was almost to the door.

Beth grabbed the napkin, wiped her face, and blew her nose.

"Thanks, Jim. You're right!"

With that, she bolted out of her chair and ran toward the departing James.

"Stop! James, please stop!"

Hearing his name, he was turning around when Beth came flying into his arms.

"Oh James," she cried, "I thought I'd never see you again!"

Congratulating himself for not sabotaging the reunion, Jim quietly slipped away and went back to work.

Chapter 76

Time has a way of settling old wounds. After three months of watching his mom and James working on dissolving long-standing accusations, bruised egos, broken promises, and smashed hearts, and as soon as James's divorce from Cora was granted, Jim was glad when they slipped off to Las Vegas and came back a married couple.

Enough money works miracles, and that's what it had taken to get rid of Cora, his fourth. She was one of his ex-wives who would never need to work two jobs to survive.

Of course, the honeymoon would take place on his yacht that had been manned by a skeleton crew while James was gone. And, of course, that would happen as soon as all evidence of his other wives had been removed. Beth was adamant about that one.

Jim and Addie had first turned down the invitation to accompany them on their honeymoon. When James finally convinced them that the yacht was so large they wouldn't have to even bump into each other unless they wanted to, they accepted the offer and hastily applied for passports.

*****

While Michigan enjoys less than a hundred days of full sun a year, in this part of the world the sun shows its face three hundred days.

Enjoying the warm temperatures, Jim and Addie held hands at the back of the tender and watched the port city of Barcelona fade into the background. As the tender plowed its way through the Mediterranean Sea on its way to James's yacht, Addie marveled at the way things had turned out. Maybe she had to go through the experience of being ditched by Steve and conned by Earl to appreciate the man sitting next to her.

But one thing troubled her about their relationship. Ever since the day in his office when she'd offered her body as payment for feeling safe, Jim had changed. Oh, she had no doubt that he loved her because she could see it. The problem was his lack of returned passion when she kissed him. He didn't feel *that way* about her.

Evelyn Allen Harper
*****

As the tender sped through the blue water, Jim could see his dad's yacht in the distance. How was he ever going to keep his hands off Addie when there would be just the two of them alone with each other for ten days? It had taken more control than he thought he had and dozens of cold showers, but he had done it. He had courted her like a gentleman from the Puritanical days, and even though she was demanding more, he stuck to his resolve. Until he felt that she loved him completely, that's as far as he would allow it to go; he wasn't settling for anything less.

*****

It was morning, three days into their vacation when Jim felt warm breath on his neck as he stood by the ship's rail watching the waves lap against the side of the yacht.

"Good morning, Addie," he said through clenched jaws. She was going to be the death of him.

Addie didn't reply.

Warm lips sucked on his earlobe.

"Ready for breakfast?" he asked in a husky voice.

The warm lips moved to his mouth and Addie pressed her body against his.

"I'm really hungry," he mumbled as he pushed her away.

Addie dropped her arms and stepped back. If that's how he felt, then she was fed up. With her hands on her hips, she faced him. "Okay, Jim, I get it, and I quit."

"You quit? What in the world are you talking about?"

"I quit trying to get a reaction out of you. You say you love me, and I believe you, but I want more than you're willing to give."

"What? Not willing? Addie if you only knew."

Addie shook her head and continued. "You keep holding me away, treating me as if I'd break if you hugged me too hard or kissed me too passionately. I really had hoped that things would change once we were at sea, but they haven't. It's obvious that you don't feel *that way* about me, so I give up." Holding back tears, she turned and stomped away.

"Addie," he said quietly, "please stay."

Addie whipped around, angry. "Why? Why should I stay? Are things going to change?"

"Do you love me, Addie?"

218

Sweet Adeline

"With all my heart, Jim. And that's what so sad about all of this."

Jim's heart soared. She'd said the magic words! She loved him. The months of holding her at arm's length waiting for her to fall in love with him were over. Turning her down again and again had been some of the hardest things he had ever done. He wanted to build the foundation with her that could stand the test of time, not something fleeting like he had watched her have with Steve and Earl.

His hand reached into his pocket to find the object he'd been carrying around since they boarded the yacht. Now was the time.

Before he could say anything, she walked away.

"Addie, turn around."

Looking straight ahead, she answered, "No, I mean it. If our relationship to you is nothing more than lukewarm, I'm moving on."

"Addie, turn around!"

Huffing a sigh of resignation, she looked back to see Jim down on one knee looking up at her. In his hand was a ring.

Jim looked into her startled green eyes and forgot his carefully rehearsed speech. Instead all he could think to say was, "Addie, will you marry me?"

She didn't hesitate for a second to blurt out her answer.

"No."

"No?"

"No."

His mouth dropped open. "But I thought—"

"Were you going to say that now that you know I truly love you, I would accept your ring?"

"Was I wrong to think that? Please, give me a clue, Addie, because now I'm completely confused."

"Jim, I'm not saying that you don't love me, because I know you do. It's just that I refuse to enter into a passionless marriage."

"What?" he yelled. "How can you even think that? Since we've been together, I've taken so many cold showers that my skin gets puckery just thinking about it. Being near you turns me into mush, and when you kiss me, it takes all the strength in my body not to grab you and haul you off to bed."

When she just stared at him stunned, he continued.

Evelyn Allen Harper

"Keeping my hands off you is killing me, Addie. I guess I should have given you my speech before I asked you to marry me."

She finally grinned. "Your speech? Did you rehearse it?"

He nodded, his face flaming with embarrassment.

"Could I hear it now? Give me the speech and then ask me again."

Kneeling down on one knee, he took a breath and looked into her green eyes.

"Addie, I've loved you since the first time I laid eyes on you. You have no idea how much I've suffered working so close to you without being allowed to touch you. It was hard the two years you were with Steve, but that was mild compared to the desperation I felt when you hooked up Earl and I knew I couldn't compete with him. But my love never wavered. I dreamed constantly of being with you. I love you, Addie, and I will forever love you."

His whole body was shaking when it came time for the question.

"Addie," he asked in a shaky voice, scared to death to hear the answer, "will you marry me?"

"Oh, yes! Yes!" Her eyes filled with tears as he slipped the ring on her finger.

Relieved, he pulled her into a tight hug and kissed her soundly. "I was just waiting until I was sure you love me as much as I love you."

"Oh Jim, I had given up on us!"

He groaned. "Lawson men only love one woman in their lives and you, my sweet Adeline, are mine."

She giggled. "I'm engaged and I want to tell the whole world, but I'm stuck miles away from shore. If I shout it from the deck in the direction of Monte Carlo, do you think they'd hear me?"

"No silly girl, I don't even think my parents would hear you on the other side of the yacht!"

"We've got to do something to celebrate, Jim! Any ideas?"

Jim's eyes lit up. "I do have one suggestion."

"What? Go swimming in the warm Mediterranean Sea?" Addie grinned, waiting.

He pulled her close and kissed the tip of her nose. "We are going to play a game called *Follow the Leader*."

"Oh, I remember that game. Can I be the leader?"

"No, since it's my idea, I get to be the leader."

220

Sweet Adeline

"Says who?"

"Says me."

Addie's laughing face took away the sting of her next question. "Are you always going to be so bossy? Jeeze! Maybe I should rethink this marriage bit."

Jim chuckled. "Ah, come on. Humor me! You'll love where I'm going to take you."

She looked at him for a moment, pretending indecision. "Okay, Mr. Self-Elected-Leader. I'll play your silly game, but I get to pick the next one and make the rules."

"Duly noted! But you're going to have trouble coming up with something as good as this one. Addie, I promise you're not going to be disappointed."

"Well, then, lead on!"

Jim took off at a fast pace.

"Slow down!" Addie pleaded. "I can't keep up with your long legs!"

"It's just that I'm *really* anxious to get there, so hurry up."

"There? Give me a clue."

Jim opened his mouth prepared to say, "My bed!" when he heard his mother's voice calling from an upper deck.

"Hello, you two!"

Jim and Addie came to an abrupt halt.

"Mom?" Jim questioned.

"James, I found them!" Beth yelled.

"I'll be right there," James called back.

"Mom, what's going on?" Jim couldn't believe what was happening.

"There's nothing going on. It's just that we haven't seen the two of you since we boarded the ship. If you don't have other plans, would you two consider having breakfast with us?"

Other plans? Of course he had other plans! Jim was trying hard to hide his frustration. Why, oh why, had his mother chosen to show up now?

Addie, who had no idea where he was taking her, looked pleased. "We really weren't doing anything, well, I can't say that because we were in the middle of a game of *Follow the Leader*."

Beth looked puzzled. "Are you having trouble finding activities on board?"

"On, no! Jim just wanted to play a new game."

"Are you enjoying life on the yacht?"

"Very much so!" Turning to Jim, Addie whispered, "Should we tell them that we're engaged?"

Beth's eyes widened. "Did I hear the word engaged?"

Jim relaxed. Might as well accept the fact that it wasn't going to happen. He reached out, gathered her in his arms, and kissed her soundly. "Yes," he said to his mother, "Addie and I are engaged!"

"Oh, there you are!" James called out to Beth. "You found them?"

"Yes, I did! James, our son is engaged!"

"Great! That's good news, Son!"

Turning to Beth he asked, "Did they say they'd have breakfast with us?"

Jim called to his dad, "We'll see you in the dining room."

"Good," James called back. "Come on, Beth. I'm starved."

Addie turned to Jim. "Guess our *Follow the Leader* game will have to wait. Where were you taking me, anyway?"

God, he loved this woman! "You'll have to wait until after breakfast to find out."

"Promise?"

"I promise."

Jim gazed at the girl he had dreamed about for years and realized there was no rush. After breakfast would be fine.

It was his turn.

Sweet Adeline

Writing is a lonely and almost God-like occupation. The writer fills his imaginary world with living breathing characters who have names, attributes, and personalities and then, like God, has the power to choose which of them will succeed, which ones will have their heart's broken and which ones won't make it to the end of the story.

Writing might be a lonely occupation, but it's an exciting one.

The writing bug didn't bite me until I was well into retirement. But once it bit, it became an obsession. A day without writing, to me, is a day without sunshine. I had never written a short story, but once I started, I couldn't stop. The first venture into my new hobby was writing six books in The Accidental Mystery Series, followed by a two book series, The Coat and The Collar.

I have a circle of friends who not only are very supportive, they also keep my feet planted firmly on the ground with their sharp red correcting pencils. Every time I tell them I've written yet another book, a few of them roll their eyes. I think I'm wearing them out.

While in the process of writing Sweet Adeline, I sent sections as I finished them to Judy Freed, Judith Wishin, Pat Bell, and Karen Fritz. Karen is my Word Person who does her best to make it look as if I'm somewhat intelligent. The editor at Ink Smith, Corinne Anderson, worked her magic, and the story is much better because of her.

The cover of Sweet Adeline was created by Macy Stom. She is a freelance artist and graphic designer, working closely with Ink Smith Publishing. She pulled the cover together—giving Addie's personality a perfect visual.

All authors love feedback, and I'm no exception. You can contact me at evharp@gmail.com, and I promise to answer your email.